CHRISTA JAUSSI

Brother's Keeper

First published by Kindle Direct Publishing 2019

First edition

Editing by Rachel Harris

*This book was professionally typeset on Reedsy.
Find out more at reedsy.com*

Dedicated to my brother and best friend
Blake Eggett
December 4, 1987 - October 28, 2005

Foreword

Every single person makes choices. No one is exempt from this daily experience. Some choices become habits that we focus very little on, and some choices take days, weeks, months, or even years to make. These choices shape us and those around us, whether we know it or not. Some choices are small, and some are the kind that can change your life forever.

Chapter 1

J ordyn heard screaming. She soon realized that the painfully loud screeching was coming from her own mouth. She had run into this unfamiliar bathroom to be alone fifteen minutes ago, but it felt like time was standing still. Jordyn reached for the large roll of toilet paper on the vanity counter to wipe her face. This house belonged to Debra, her neighbor and mother's best friend. Debra, along with Jordyn's big brother, Brady, had brought her here right after school had ended earlier that day. Using all her strength to stand up from the edge of the bathtub, Jordyn looked into the brass-trimmed mirror. All she saw looking back at her were red eyes with black mascara running down her face. It had smeared all over without her even realizing it since she had locked herself in here. Looking like a scary clown would have never been okay normally, but she was satisfied that she looked as awful as she felt inside.

Jordyn took a deep breath and held it in. As she slowly let the air out of her mouth, she leaned against the bathroom door trying to compose herself enough to go back out. She tried to slow her breathing and looked around at the pastel pink walls. She looked right past the painting of a rabbit and straight out the window where even the sky looked gloomy and depressing.

Jordyn was desperate to stay locked in the bathroom forever, but she reluctantly came out of the solitude it provided and walked slowly through the hallway into the living room where Brady and Debra sat. Trying not to look anyone directly in the eyes, she walked past the couch where they were sitting and sat in a chair that was positioned in the back corner of the room. She hoped that she could stay hidden while she still tried to process everything that had just happened.

"Dad is on his way here from work now," Jordyn's mom, Kathleen, spoke from the doorway to the room at large, as if the reassurance was for herself as much as anyone.

Jordyn watched her mother walk into the living room from the kitchen where she had been making phone calls to family members and their church clergy. Jordyn had overheard some of what she was saying, but she was too wrapped up in her own thoughts that she hadn't tried very hard to make sense of it. Kathleen sat down in a wooden rocking chair next to the couch and closed her eyes tightly, keeping them shut for a few minutes. The grieving mother didn't want to leave them all alone, but she also needed to somehow deal with her own thoughts and feelings.

Kathleen barely reached five feet tall, so her feet only touched the floor when the chair rocked forward. Jordyn didn't get a lack of height from Kathleen, as she was a proud five-foot eight, but they were similar in many other ways. People often mistook Jordyn for her mother over the phone and they both had a quiet but fierce laugh. If only they could be laughing right now instead.

The room was silent for a while, but the quiet was welcomed by all four people. There wasn't much that could be said by any one of them right now and no one tried to figure out how to break the silence. Jordyn was appreciating the fact that no one had commented on her time in the bathroom or on her still mascara-stained face, until she remembered that she was supposed to be at work right now. She contemplated staying in her corner and pushing the thought out of her mind, but she decided to say something.

"Mom, I'm supposed to be cleaning the elementary school right now. What should I do?" Her voice came out a little shaky.

Kathleen opened her eyes and softly spoke, "We can call them tomorrow and explain. It will be fine."

"Okay." Jordyn was fine remaining in her safe corner.

Brady's friend was in charge of the cleaning crew. He offered, "I could call Peter and explain what's happening. That way you can just not worry about going in for a few weeks."

Jordyn looked up for the first time since she ran into the bathroom, giving a thankful nod and look to Brady. Somehow, her brother Brady always knew what to do and say just like a big brother should. Brady, like all of her brothers, was taller than she was, but unlike her other brothers, Brady had a strong, broad build.

She wondered how Brady could be so helpful right now and not a complete mess like she obviously was. Jordyn kept a close eye on him and watched as he bravely made the phone call in her stead. He looked sad as he talked quietly and slowly and began to pace back and forth by the window next to the front door, but he was being strong—by controlling his emotions and doing the hard things that had to be done—by explaining a horrible situation in a concise way and then the strength to hang up and keep his emotions in check.

It was that same strength Jordyn had witnessed just a half hour ago from him when he had picked her up from school with Debra. Brady ran out of Debra's car to Jordyn waiting out on the grass. He had immediately given her the most loving and powerfully expressive hug—without any words between them, Jordyn knew with her whole being that there was something terribly wrong. Brady guided her to their neighbor's worn down silver Toyota and opened the right-side passenger door for her to climb in before going around to the other side to get in beside her.

On their way to Debra's home, Jordyn pleaded over and over to Brady, "Tell me what's going on right now. I need to know what's happening. Can you *please* just tell me what's happening?"

With all the strength Brady had, he had waited to tell her any details until Debra pulled into her driveway. Brady was strong again when he let Jordyn fall apart in his arms after he finally told her what had happened. If she had to describe him in one word, Jordyn would describe Brady as *strength*.

The flash of the front door opening brought Jordyn back into the present moment. She looked over to see her dad, Fred, walking in, who was quickly met by Kathleen. As soon as he set foot into the house, they disappeared through the hallway together. Jordyn guessed they had gone to an empty bedroom to talk. Jordyn kept quiet in the chair in the corner. It was a haven for her at the moment because she could just sit there in silence without worry. A numbing feeling was taking over her after feeling such extreme pain and anguish. She traced the floral patterns on the chair with her index finger while she attempted to stop thinking. The time didn't pass very quickly and it felt like it was probably an hour since her parents had disappeared.

Jordyn's parents finally came back into the main living area where everyone else was waiting. The whole day felt long and all Jordyn wanted to do was to go home to a familiar place to lie down. Her unmade blankets on her bed from that morning would be the most welcoming sight to her. She felt a little uncomfortable in Debra's house since she hadn't really spent much time there before, and what she really wanted was to go to her own room where she could have real privacy to cry uncontrollably for as long as necessary without anyone else around.

Bravely, she spoke up, "Mom, can we go home now?"

"No, I'm sorry." Kathleen said disappointingly.

"How much longer until we can?"

Fred took the hard question, trying to give his wife a reprieve from having to be the one handling everything.

"The police are there still, so we can't let you go home. We actually think it would be best if you stayed the night at Livie's house."

"No, please. I just want to go home!"

"Honey, I know you do. We don't want you to have to see the house right now and have bad memories from it until the police are all done."

Jordyn wanted to keep fighting it, but she didn't have the energy. Not entirely sure how much time had passed, she suddenly saw Livie at the door, ready to walk together to her house. Livie was one of her best friends and was always so sweet and kind to everyone she came in contact with. Jordyn hugged her friend, but hoped she didn't want to talk about anything. Livie seemed to read her mind, because she allowed for silence as they started walking the two blocks to her house. Two small dogs at the house on the corner always came right up to the fence and barked loudly whenever anyone passed by. Today was no exception as the dogs ran up at full-speed, jumping up to the top of the five-foot chain-link fence and barking at Livie and Jordyn. It was strangely reassuring to Jordyn to still have something she could count on in life—even if those dogs had always been annoying to her.

When they arrived at the Hansen's modest blue rambler, dinner was already on the table. No one quite knew what topics to talk about during dinner, so the only things that were exchanged that evening were hugs and tears. Jordyn didn't know what to say to anyone, either. There were so many thoughts and emotions running through her and there was no way to navigate through them. She didn't even know the whole situation herself, but she wanted to figure out more before she started talking to anyone about what had happened.

Even though it was a Friday night and they didn't have to wake up early for school, Jordyn had no desire to stay up any later than she had to. Right after dinner was all cleaned up, she exhaustedly went downstairs into Livie's bedroom. She didn't have any of her things with her, so Livie's mom, Tina, gave her a new toothbrush from their linen closet and Livie let her sleep in one of her comfortable t-shirts and basketball shorts. It was difficult for Jordyn not to even have her own pillow and blanket to snuggle up in and give her comfort when she felt so lost and heartbroken.

To finish off the night, Jordyn finally washed off all the mascara left on her face from earlier. Her eyes were still red, and when she saw herself in the mirror, she looked like a completely different person than she had that morning. There was an emptiness in her eyes, and Jordyn wasn't sure she was even really seeing herself.

They climbed into Livie's queen-sized bed and Jordyn laid

her head back onto a pillow that wasn't hers, pulling a blanket up to her chin that didn't smell like home. Nothing about today felt real. She pinched herself just to make sure that it was, indeed, all reality. They said goodnight to each other and Jordyn thought that she would have a hard time falling asleep. Or maybe better—she would never wake up, or would wake up tomorrow and find that it was all one crazy, awful nightmare. Ever since Jordyn was little, her parents had taught her to pray to her Father in Heaven before falling asleep, but she was sure that tonight she wouldn't be blamed if she passed on it. She closed her eyes, determined to fall asleep without praying, but Jordyn could hear her parents in her mind sweetly reminding her to pray as if she were still a little girl. She said a very general, fast prayer because she didn't feel ready for a heart-to-heart with God yet, either.

Blake, her closest brother, had taken his own life earlier that day. How could she face the rest of her life when she had lost him to suicide?

Jordyn's eyes closed from exhaustion, and she fell asleep instantly.

Chapter 2

Morning came too quickly. As Jordyn sat up in Livie's bed, everything came flooding back to her. For the ten hours she was asleep, she was able to forget that Blake was gone. But immediately upon waking up, she remembered; her stomach hurt and her heart ached for him. Livie had already gotten out of bed and gone upstairs for breakfast, so Jordyn was alone—finally alone. Jordyn lowered her body back down onto the bed and closed her eyes again. Wanting to fall back asleep so she could escape the heaviness she felt, she lay still for a long time. Unfortunately, Jordyn felt more awake than she had ever felt in a morning and couldn't stop all of the thoughts that were running through her mind. One after another, the thoughts raced around and around until she jumped out of the bed.

Maybe being alone right now isn't what I want after all.

Jordyn reached for her clothes on the long white dresser and began changing into them. First, she pulled on her black v-neck shirt over her naturally curly brown hair. But then she stopped mid-reach when she saw her olive khaki skirt. The skirt was brand new, and yesterday had been the first time she had worn it. Jordyn picked it up and sat on the pink-checkered comforter on the bed, just staring at her skirt. Yesterday, this skirt represented getting all dressed up and cute for Greg, her school crush. Jordyn had liked Greg ever since she had met him three years ago. He was tall, athletic, and the kind of person everyone wanted to be friends with. She was about to turn sixteen in a month, which was when she could start dating, and it was no secret who she wanted her first date to be with. But today—today, that skirt just represented the worst day of her life. She decided to tuck the skirt into her backpack and ask Livie if she could borrow her basketball shorts for the day. Seeing that Livie was probably the nicest girl she'd ever met, Jordyn was positive it would be just fine.

Slowly, Jordyn started up the stairs that led into the kitchen and found only Tina eating cereal at the table. She could see the rest of Livie's family out the back window, raking up the fall leaves. Out of habit, Jordyn walked around the table and sat in the chair she normally used when she ate with the Hansens. As she sat down on the wooden kitchen chair across from Tina, she placed her backpack in her lap.

"What would you like for breakfast, sweetie?" Tina was always so hospitable when Jordyn came over to their house. Jordyn admired this woman's sweet nature that she must have passed on to Livie.

"I'm okay. I'm really not feeling very good."

"Are you sure I can't get you anything?"

"Really, I'm okay. Have you heard from my mom yet?"

"Yes, good news! I actually just got off the phone with her. She said that I should bring you home as soon as you're ready."

"I'd rather just walk myself home if that's alright with you. And I'm ready now." Jordyn squeezed her backpack extra tight.

Reluctantly, Tina gave Jordyn an unsure but understanding nod, smiling softly.

"Thank you for letting me stay here. Will you tell Livie goodbye for me?"

With the same soft smile, Tina nodded again. It took everything Jordyn had inside of her to not let out the tears that were starting to surface in the corners of her eyes. She stood up without looking Tina in the eye for fear of crying in front of her, and turned and walked through the hallway and out the front door. She walked quickly to the sidewalk and past the three tall oak trees where she wouldn't be seen by Tina, who was most likely watching Jordyn through the window. As soon as she got to the third oak tree, Jordyn slowed her pace and let the tears fall freely.

The sound of frantic barking brought her back into reality and she looked over to see the two dogs at the corner house. *Did I really just cross the street?* she thought. Jordyn looked back and was glad to see that there were no cars on the road and that she really did make it across safely. Wiping away tears, she paused to look over at the dogs jumping up and down on the fence. *Maybe they lost someone they loved and that's why they are mad all the time. Yeah. That must be it.* she decided.

Jordyn's house was in view now, and she followed the urge to run to her front door. No words could express how glad she was to be home at last. As she turned the doorknob and stepped over the threshold, she heard unfamiliar voices in her house. She heard her mom's voice call down in a friendly tone.

"Hey, honey. Bishop Johnson and his wife are here visiting us. Why don't you come upstairs and say hello?"

Yet another obstacle prevented Jordyn from being able to completely melt down in her bedroom. Her knee-jerk reaction was to rush down the stairs toward her room instead of the ones going up to more people.

Kathleen could sense Jordyn's hesitancy and called down again, "Jordyn? Come be with us."

Kathleen wasn't outspoken very often, so it was always a good idea to obey when she was. Slowly but surely, Jordyn came up the stairs—ready or not.

"I'm really glad we caught you at home, Jordyn," Sister Johnson said with sincerity.

"Thanks." was all Jordyn could come up with in reply. Small talk hadn't ever been Jordyn's strong suit, especially now that she didn't have the energy to think of polite ways to keep the conversation going.

"Greg also wanted us to tell you how sorry he is to hear about Blake and that he is thinking of you."

No words came out and she tried to keep from blushing, but Jordyn was sure that it was obvious how much she liked to hear that. Bishop Johnson was one of their church leaders, the equivalent to a pastor. Jordyn looked up to him and his wife for how strong and caring they were, and it helped that they were the great people who had brought Greg into the world. For a brief moment, Jordyn was lost in thoughts about Greg, but then she realized that meant that other people now knew about Blake's suicide and were probably talking about it. They all had to find out about it at some point, but she didn't really like the thought of that. It felt too real.

"Would you like that, Jordyn?" Kathleen asked expectantly.

Jordyn hadn't realized that they all had kept talking while she had been thinking about everything.

"Sorry, what?"

"Would you like a blessing from Bishop Johnson?"

"Oh, sure. Thank you."

Bishop Johnson, Jordyn's father, and Brady all stood in a

circle around her, laying their hands softly on her head. Bishop Johnson began giving a beautiful blessing to Jordyn—that she could have peace, find answers to her questions, have the comfort she needed, and be able to stay close to her family who loved her. Jordyn felt a tear on her arm, but this time she didn't care that other people could see her crying. She had held it all in for too long, and it was as if the tears erupted out of her like a dam finally being released. Even though she wasn't concerned about anyone else in the room, Jordyn heard sniffling sounds other than just hers and could tell that there were more tears than just her own.

Jordyn's heart hurt so much that it was hard for her to identify the tiniest feeling of love during the blessing amid all her pain. The blessing opened the anguish she was trying to keep all locked up inside and she felt the most awful feelings coming over her.

Why did Blake leave me?

Why didn't I know he was in so much pain?

What could I have done to keep him here?

Why wasn't I enough to help him feel love?

Why?

Feeling like she just had the wind knocked out of her, Jordyn couldn't take it any longer. Not even caring if it was impolite, she stood up in the middle of the blessing circle and stumbled down the two flights of stairs to her bedroom. In the hallway, she paused when she saw Blake's door next to hers. Instead of going into her bedroom, she walked to his and fell onto his bed with her face down in his pillow. As Jordyn took a deep breath trying to calm herself, she could distinctly smell Blake. She held her breath in as long as she could to try and keep the smell with her forever. Unable to hold her breath very long due to her uncontrollable sobbing, she repeated smelling his pillow over and over again.

As she lay there, Jordyn could feel warmth all around her. Blake felt close to her and she could just picture him sitting on the chair next to the bed. Two days ago, she was laying in that exact spot while he was sitting on the chair playing a game. Jordyn turned over facing the ceiling and kept her eyes closed as she pictured that moment with him. They had been talking about school and the math class they were both in. They had made a plan to study together and Blake had been alleviating her doubts that she'd do fine on the test next week. Jordyn had reached for the math book on his desk when she had seen a piece of paper with her name on it. Before she could read it, Blake had hurriedly taken it away from her and told her she couldn't read it yet.

Quickly, Jordyn sat up on the bed as she remembered the paper that Blake had hidden away in his desk drawer from her. She reached for the desk drawer with great anticipation, but Jordyn was also nervous about what she would find. Sure enough, on top of a stack of papers was a letter with her name written all over it. As she reached for it to read it, her head collapsed into her hands as she was overcome with emotions—gratitude, fear, happiness, and sadness.

It took a minute, but Jordyn finally gathered herself enough to take the paper out of the desk and read it. It was a note to her and Blake's best friend, Benson.

I hereby leave Jordyn in the care of Benson Alby. Benson will need to watch over, protect, and tease Jordyn as much as possible.

Of course Blake would be making jokes in his note.

I trust Jordyn in your care. So it is written, so it is done.
   Signed, Blake

The tears that followed reading this note were the purest and truest sorrowful tears that Jordyn had ever shed. Jordyn couldn't believe that she wouldn't hear Blake joke the way he did in that note ever again. She couldn't believe that she wouldn't have her best friend next door to rely on anymore. Jordyn could, however, believe that Blake would be thoughtful enough to make sure she was cared for. The sweet note he had left for her also made Jordyn angry at him. She wanted him to be the one to take care of her—not anyone else.

Jordyn heard the front door close and realized that the Johnsons must have left. She picked up the note from Blake and left his room to go into her own. Jordyn determinedly pulled some papers off of her push-pin board and threw them onto the ground carelessly. She carefully pinned up Blake's note next to a picture of them playing mini-golf on the cruise ship from their family vacation the previous summer.

Content that she had done and felt enough for that day, Jordyn made her way over to her bed and pulled all of her own cozy and familiar blankets over her shoulders and rolled onto her side into the fetal position. It was time to forget about reality again as she drifted off to sleep for a quick escape.

Chapter 3

Everyone was busy getting ready for the funeral. There were people to contact, the funeral service to plan, the obituary to write, pictures to be gathered, and everyone Jordyn's family knew (and some they didn't know) to visit with while they offered food and gifts. On top of all of that, Brady was getting ready to leave on his church mission a week after the funeral. Jordyn couldn't believe that he was still planning on going. Jordyn had five older brothers, but Brady was now the only one left at home with her. After he left, she would be there alone with her parents, which she was dreading. It was nothing against her parents, but she was quickly realizing that she didn't like to be alone. Their house was constantly full of people right now, people which were a blessed distraction for Jordyn. She liked keeping busy with everyone to help quiet her own thoughts.

"Hey, favorite sister!"

Trevor, Jordyn's second oldest brother, greeted her in the kitchen while she was helping their mom set the table for dinner. All of her brothers would call her their favorite since she was the only girl, and Jordyn adored it.

"Oh, hi! I didn't realize you were coming today. I'm glad you're here."

Trevor was quite a bit taller than Jordyn, and as he hugged her, he lowered his head to touch the top of hers. He and his wife were the last ones to join them at dinner that evening since they had to come from out of state. One by one, Trevor went around the house and talked to the family and friends that were there, although most people had left their house by now.

Twenty minutes went by, and the last few people trickled out the door to leave for the evening. It was now just the immediate family sitting around the table to eat dinner together. Fred offered a prayer to bless the food, and they all began to dish up the chicken and potatoes that Debra had brought over for them to eat.

"This smells delicious. I'm so hungry!" Nate called as he stepped into the kitchen.

Nate, Jordyn's oldest brother, always had a busy work schedule but was finally able to come over for dinner tonight to be with the family.

"Me too, Nate. Don't take it all like you usually do! Will you hand me the pepper, Brady?" Dillon joined right in.

Dillon had always been the funny one in the family. He was born between Trevor and Brady and did well as a middle child. He helped connect all the family together with his humor and light-hearted spirit.

During the small talk and chatting, the front door opened and Jordyn's ears perked up as she heard footsteps coming up the stairs. Her heart sunk deep into her chest when she realized that she had expected it to be Blake coming around the corner into the kitchen for dinner. Instead, it was Jordyn's aunt coming back for her purse. The disappointment Jordyn felt was a punch to the gut and almost felt as if she had just found out for the first time that he was gone. Blake would never walk through that front door ever again. He would never try to scare her as she turned around the corner downstairs anymore. He would never again make a silly face to her from across the lunchroom at school. He would never poke her as they were kneeling during family prayer. He would never be there.

"Jordyn, can you pass the butter to me?" Fred asked his daughter.

Jordyn paused as memories were still flooding through her mind.

"Blake would have pretended to throw the butter to you because you said to *pass* the butter."

All eyes turned to Jordyn and the conversation ceased. No one had dared to bring Blake up in conversation yet tonight. Bringing up Blake was like stepping through a minefield because no one knew how anyone would react, but Jordyn didn't care.

"He will never do that again," Jordyn plainly stated.

After a moment, she looked blankly forward through everyone's stares, adding, "He is gone."

Everyone was completely silent—no one even shifted in their chairs.

Finally, Fred spoke to alleviate the tension. "Yes, he is gone, and I miss him too."

Feeling complete emptiness well up inside of her, Jordyn didn't talk during the rest of dinner. A few of her brothers discussed what Brady still needed to buy for his two-year church service mission, and offered to go shopping with him. Jordyn just sat and built her mashed potatoes into different shapes while they talked and ate. Once again, she wasn't feeling very hungry, but every so often she would take little bites of food so she didn't draw extra attention to herself.

While Jordyn was getting ready for bed that night, she couldn't help but think how horrible her life was now. Just a few days ago, she had felt on top of the world and like nothing could get in her way. How was it possible that things could change so quickly? Not only did she feel awful and hopeless, but Jordyn also couldn't see how that feeling would ever change for her. Blake was never coming back. If that was true, then she would always feel this way. Jordyn couldn't see a way around it.

As Jordyn set her phone on her nightstand and grabbed the charger to plug it in, her hand touched her scriptures. She gently ran her fingers over the top of them. Hesitantly, she grabbed them and opened to her bookmark in the book of John where her class had been studying in Seminary. Her eyes focused on the bookmark—it had a picture of the Savior on it. She remembered the discussion they had in class just that past week on how Jesus can help us in everything we are feeling and experiencing. Her teacher spoke so passionately about it and challenged them at the end of class to ask Jesus for help with something during the next week. Jordyn had already done the challenge and prayed for help when she studied for a test, but now she didn't know how to even begin asking for help on this. It was so big and heavy. All Jordyn had the energy to do right now was to hope it was true. Maybe she could think about it more while she was sitting in church tomorrow. Jordyn closed her scriptures without reading any of the verses and went to sleep.

* * *

All eyes were on Jordyn's family as they walked down the aisle to a bench near the front of the chapel. Brady was giving the traditional farewell talk today before leaving on his mission, and it seemed like the whole city had caught news of Blake's suicide and showed up to support their family.

Here Brady goes again—showing strength by facing all of these people right now, Jordyn thought as she watched him talk to a few people on his way up to his seat. It was hard for her to know how to feel when they hadn't even had Blake's funeral yet. *Did everyone know about his suicide? Were they all looking at her and feeling sorry for her? What must they be thinking about her family right now?*

Jordyn could feel the tan brick walls closing in on her and felt that she was too tightly confined in the chapel. As the panic was overtaking her and right as she was about to stand up and walk out of the chapel for some fresh air, she caught a glimpse of Greg and his parents sitting on a bench nearby. Greg's dark chocolate brown eyes met hers and in an instant, Jordyn's heartbeats slowed down and she was able to take a deep breath and feel calm. Greg gave Jordyn a smile of encouragement and Jordyn's eyes started to shine with water filling them. Jordyn looked away from Greg just in time before the tears fell down her cheeks. She tried to quickly wipe them away before other people could see.

Bishop Johnson walked away from his family on the bench. As he made his way up to his place on the stand for the meeting to begin, he first stopped and shook Jordyn's parents' hands.

"Thank you so much for your dedication in being here. Supporting one son while grieving for another must be difficult. Everyone here today is going to benefit from your family's example." He said quietly to them. The bishop then took his place on the stand, and the meeting began.

The Sunday service was emotional for everyone there. When

Brady finished speaking, there were no dry faces in the whole church building. After the talk ended, Jordyn remembered that she and Blake were supposed to do a musical number together. She had learned how to play the flute so she could be just like her big brother. They would play together regularly in church or for family, and she enjoyed practicing with him. Jordyn was grateful that no one expected her to play today without him.

The funeral was only two days away, and she hoped to find the courage to play the flute during the service since it was the only way she knew how to honor Blake. She wasn't sure how tears and blowing into a flute would go, but she was hoping that she could pull it off. In past performances, Blake would normally carry them through the song, so it would be more than challenging to do it without him.

* * *

To the dread of the whole family, the morning of the funeral came all too soon. Jordyn would usually get ready by curling her hair nicely and putting on makeup, but she had no desire to get ready today. She pulled her hair back into a ponytail and put on her plain black dress. The only funeral she had been to was for her Grandpa when she was seven, so she didn't quite know what to expect but she did remember people wearing black in the movies. Jordyn wasn't ready to say goodbye or to really even accept that Blake was dead, but attending his funeral seemed like it required her to do both. Ready or not, she had to go upstairs and head over to the church building with her family to the funeral.

During the viewing right before the funeral, Jordyn saw her parents graciously greet all their loved ones. *How could they carry an optimistic smile and be hugging and comforting other people when they were grieving right now?* Then Jordyn looked over at a family coming through the receiving line that she didn't recognize. They had three small children. As she watched the mother rocking their young baby in her arms, Jordyn started to feel angry inside.

Look at this normal family, she thought. How she longed to feel normal inside. Jordyn frowned as the next thought came into her mind. *I hope none of those children ever cause that family any sort of grief like this. Stay young and happy, little ones.*

Everyone except for the immediate family was excused from the viewing room just before the funeral was about to start. Jordyn's whole family went up to the casket and gathered for a family prayer. Jordyn didn't close her eyes or focus on the words of the prayer. All she could do was stare at Blake's face. This was the first time she had seen him since Friday morning before he died, and everything felt so real to her at this moment. He really was dead. It wasn't all a bad dream like she had hoped. There was no need to pinch herself because she knew with absoluteness that this was her reality now.

Everyone in the church stood up as Jordyn's family walked into the chapel to sit in the front row. Jordyn didn't dare look around at who was there as she walked, so she kept her eyes on Brady's feet in front of her. His brand new dress shoes didn't distract Jordyn enough, though, and she could feel everyone's eyes on her and her family.

Messages of hope and seeing her brother again in Heaven were the theme of the funeral. Jordyn watched as her father cried through a great talk he gave about Blake and how they would all be together as a family forever. Still, Jordyn couldn't help but feel so depressed through it all. She knew that the promise of eternal families was true, and had even felt Blake really near to her since his suicide, but nothing anyone said could make her feel any better today.

It was finally her turn for the musical number. Trevor and his wife were accompanying her during a rendition of "Amazing Grace." Jordyn grabbed the flute under the bench and started following them up where she would stand by the piano and play. She didn't ask her parents' permission, but she had grabbed Blake's flute from his room instead of using her own. She fiddled her fingers on the flute keys as she walked. She then placed her lips on the mouthpiece to gently blow warm air into the cold flute.

Jordyn walked up the four steps to the stand and rounded the corner behind the music stand. She faced toward the crowd of people for the very first time. Her breath was taken away when she saw people packing the church from the chapel through the gym and onto the stage in the back. Jordyn couldn't believe what she was witnessing. How could one person have such an impact on this many people? How could Blake not have known that everyone would miss him? Jordyn wondered if he was up in Heaven crying during the funeral right along with them.

Trying to pull herself together in order to play the musical number, Jordyn looked over at Trevor. She turned her music stand toward him so she didn't have to look out at the huge crowd of people anymore. For the first time since she found out about Blake being gone, Jordyn said a real prayer. She silently pleaded that she would be able to make it through this song, somehow. Jordyn closed her eyes long enough to take a slow breath in and let it out. The piano music started and she had eight measures to count out until she had to blow into Blake's flute calmly enough for beautiful music to come out.

Jordyn somehow began to play right when she was supposed to. Her fingers felt light and she felt the music flow out of her in a way it normally didn't. She had a certain clarity of mind as she read the notes and her fingers matched it every step of the way. Jordyn held out the last note as long as she could until the tears caught up with her and she couldn't stop them. She had just had a small miracle and knew that Blake was doing his part to carry her through just like he always had done before.

For the rest of the funeral services, the tears wouldn't stop coming down. She thought eventually they would stop—but they didn't. When they got home, Jordyn went down into her room for the rest of the day. She pulled out her brown leather journal and her favorite pen and started writing to try and get all of her feelings out about this awful day.

November 1

My tears stain the face that once was filled with laughter.
I had no choice.
They just came out.
My heart aches at every moment
When my thoughts wander into memories.
I feel alone.
I can't help it.
I didn't want this change.
I would give anything to have you back.
I'm afraid to forget the sound of your voice,
The laughter that we had just a few hours before.
The thought of that gone is the reason
My face will be stained forever.

Chapter 4

Wednesday. It was the day after the funeral, and Jordyn just wanted to feel normal again. These last few days had her feeling emotions she had never felt before, and it made her miss who she had been a week ago. She didn't like seeing the emptiness in her eyes. When she looked into the mirror, instead of seeing the confidence and beauty that she used to see, she saw a shell of who she had been. Her parents said she could take the rest of the week off from school to stay home and regroup, but the last thing Jordyn wanted to do was to have too much alone time. Hopefully being back at school and back into her routine would help her to be a little more like herself again.

Jordyn grabbed her Algebra II and Biology textbooks, a jacket and lip gloss, and headed out her door to go upstairs. She paused and took five steps into Blake's room.

"I miss you." Jordyn muttered softly.

Making her way to his bed, she sat and grabbed his grey pillow and held it close to her chest.

Good, I can still smell him, she thought gratefully.

Her eye caught the shine of Blake's watch on the shelf that she had surprised him with last Christmas. Immediately, she reached her hand forward and pulled it off the shelf and into her arms full of things for school before trudging out of his room and up the stairs.

"Wow, you look lovely today." Kathleen said kindly.

Jordyn's mom was always quick to compliment her. Even though Kathleen seemed to put less emphasis on getting herself ready this morning, she still made time to try and make Jordyn feel special.

"Thanks. I wanted to get ready like I normally do for school."

"Well, you nailed it!"

It made Jordyn smile to hear her mom joke around a little bit. She could see that her mother felt the weight of the world on her shoulders ever since Friday. Who wouldn't?

Jordyn grabbed her backpack from the red brick fireplace and unzipped it. When she tried to place her books inside, there was something at the bottom preventing them from going in all the way. Jordyn reached in to figure out what was causing the problem and pulled out the olive khaki skirt. When she saw that crumpled skirt still haunting her, she wanted to scream. She held in her anger, but swiftly picked the skirt up and threw it away in the kitchen trash so it never again would have the power to remind her of the worst day of her life.

The mother and daughter walked out together into the brisk autumn breeze. Yet again, Jordyn felt another punch in her gut when she automatically waited on the passenger side of the family van that Blake drove her to school in every day. Once she realized her mistake, Jordyn silently turned to Kathleen, who was waiting by the sedan she usually drove. Jordyn tried to shake the question of how long things like this would keep happening. Determined to feel the slightest bit normal today, Jordyn shrugged it off and quickly changed her route to Kathleen's car.

25

Not missing any of this, Kathleen thoughtfully asked, "Are you sure you want to do this? We can march right back inside and make cookies and watch shows together all day long."

Jordyn was grateful for the bailout, but she was sure in her plan. "That would be good, but I need to go back to school sometime."

Jordyn held Blake's watch in her left hand as they drove to school. She gently rubbed the face of the watch back and forth with her thumb. When Kathleen turned into the school parking lot, Jordyn bent over to tuck the watch into her backpack where it would be safe and sound. As they pulled up to the curb, Jordyn looked up to see that this was the same spot where Brady and Debra had picked her up from school on Friday. She could feel the tears fighting to come to the surface of her eyes, but she could fight too—Jordyn quickly smashed her eyes shut before the tears could escape.

She let out an angry sigh and turned to give her mom a hug before stepping out of the car. As Jordyn was walking down the sidewalk to the door, she could hear the car still quietly idling nearby and knew her mom was waiting for her to go inside. Jordyn was dedicated to her plan for a normal day, so she walked as normally as she could into the school doors.

Just make it to my locker. Just make it to my locker. Just make it to my locker, Jordyn chanted to herself as she walked straight toward her locker. She had planned this out perfectly: there were only three minutes until the tardy bell, so most kids were working on getting to their classes, leaving no time to stop and talk to anyone.

When she saw her locker, Jordyn remembered that the last time she was at school, Blake was walking with her and had stopped at her locker. He had never stopped with her before, because he liked to go to the library before school to return books and check new ones out.

He knew he was leaving me so he stopped with me, Jordyn realized.

She remembered feeling drawn to watching him walk away from her locker that Friday morning. Jordyn said a quick prayer in her heart thanking God for giving her the feeling to watch Blake that morning. She was beyond thankful that she could have the memory of the very last time she saw him alive ingrained in her mind forever.

Jordyn made it to her locker without anyone stopping her or talking to her, which was a relief. She turned the dial on her combination lock, and opened it up to a torrent of notes falling out. She knelt down and picked them up one by one. Some were folded into a rectangle, some in a heart shape, and some were small and unfolded. The bell rang and she was left alone in the hallway. Jordyn scooted her back against the lockers, sliding her legs up toward her chest.

She hugged her knees tightly and began to read the notes. There were notes from Ashley, Laurie, Cassandra, Sarah, Julia, Weston, Steve, and of course Livie and Greg. There were even notes from people she didn't know had been friends with Blake. Jordyn only read through two of them before she was a complete mess. She shoved the notes back into her locker, wiped the tears from her face, and quietly headed to the school's side door.

Feeling too overwhelmed to go into her first class, Jordyn walked across the parking lot to the Seminary building to find someone to talk to. She really needed someone who could help her make sense of any of this and figured one of the gospel teachers would know better than she did.

It smelled like pumpkin spice as she stepped in through the double doors of the Seminary building. There were pumpkins and fall leaf garlands decorating the hallway. Fall was normally Jordyn's favorite time of year and usually she would be giddy looking forward to the festivities of the season, but it was hard to feel any measure of joy right now. She saw a light on in Brother Harley's office with the door open, and was grateful it was him on his prep period since he was her teacher this semester.

Not sure how to start the conversation, Jordyn knocked three times on his open door. Brother Harley turned around, looking a little startled to hear someone knocking and then doing a double-take upon seeing that it was Jordyn.

"I wasn't expecting you to be here today, Jordyn. Here—come. Take a seat."

Jordyn sat in one of the red armchairs along the wall of the office.

Brother Harley adjusted his rectangular-framed glasses and gently said, "It looks as if you've had a rough morning already. You caught me off-guard a little bit, because I was actually just compiling a list of scriptures and talks that I think could be helpful to you during this hard time."

"Oh, thanks, Brother Harley. I definitely need it. I am feeling pretty lost with all of this right now. I don't know what to do." Jordyn could barely see him now through a wall of tears welling in her eyes.

"I can't imagine how difficult it must be for you. It will probably take some time to work through it. I do know that we have a Savior who made it possible for us to feel peace and love. He will help you, I know he will." Brother Harley's voice had so much conviction in it again. Jordyn almost believed him.

"I did your assignment to ask Him for help with something, but it was just for a test at school. I'm not sure I can do it for this."

"This is a lot bigger than a test, that's true. Luckily, the principle is the same for asking Him for help on a test as for something so complex and difficult, like losing Blake. Here, let me add one more scripture to this list that I think will help you. Maybe start by studying these, and you can go from there." He offered her a sheet of paper after making his addition.

Jordyn wanted relief, so she took the paper from Brother Harley.

"You look like you may need a few minutes to just be. How about I leave you to rest here until the first period is almost over, and I can walk you to the school office to make sure you don't get an unexcused absence."

Brother Harley must have noticed the heaviness in her face. She was grateful that he cared enough to help her out so much.

* * *

Time went by way too quickly. As Brother Harley was about to leave her in the school office, he touched her shoulder and said, "Don't give up. You can do this with the Lord."

Jordyn gave him a faint smile and walked the opposite way toward her locker. With a deep breath in and out, Jordyn said to herself, "Okay, locker. Here I come." She gathered her things for the second period and closed her locker tight. The bell rang for the first period to get out and Jordyn walked quickly through the busy hallways. She gave little smiles and hellos to people as they passed, feeling like she had just accomplished the impossible as she walked into her classroom door. She had just seen people and it was okay, so she could definitely sit through Biology and listen silently for an hour and a half. She didn't have any friends in this class, which, for the first time, was a good thing.

Jordyn made her way to her desk which was on the left-hand-side of the room by the window. Their class was on the second floor, so it looked down outside toward the football field. She set her book down on her desk and slid into her seat. Just as she thought she was free from any reminders of Blake, she felt a tap on her shoulder. Jordyn turned around and saw a girl she didn't recognize.

"My name is Tessa. I'm not sure you know me, but I am in band class with Blake—was, I mean."

"Oh. Hello." Jordyn said reluctantly.

"I was at the funeral yesterday, and I just can't get over it. I'm so sad. It was *so* painful to be there and think about him. I sat right behind him in band and he let me use his pencil because I always forgot. He was so nice. Oh yeah—and also he snuck some gummy bears into class one day and shared them with me. It was really funny. The teacher never even caught us."

Jordyn couldn't believe that this girl was talking to her right now—and she wouldn't stop. All Jordyn could do was stare at Tessa in bewilderment.

"And he was kind of cute. Like, actually *really* cute."

Tessa stopped talking briefly but as Jordyn looked at her more closely, she could see it was because Tessa began crying.

"I can't believe he is gone!" Tessa fell forward onto Jordyn dramatically.

Jordyn contemplated in bitter amazement what was happening. Who could this girl be and why was she venting to *her* about missing Blake? She didn't know Tessa. Tessa didn't know her. How dare this random girl expect Jordyn to sympathize with her over a lost crush when she was his sister and was experiencing actual heartache right now?

The tardy bell rang a glorious four dings and Tessa went to her seat on the opposite side of the room from Jordyn. Jordyn hoped that that would be the strangest thing she would experience from here on out. None of this had been pleasant, but she didn't think she could handle any more of that—especially from a stranger.

Ms. Gregory started the lecture and dimmed the lights for all the students to see the PowerPoint presentation. Her voice was calming and faded into the background of Jordyn's mind. Nothing about today had been normal like she had hoped it would be. If this was her new normal, she didn't want any part of it.

Chapter 5

The next day, it was a struggle for Jordyn to get out of bed. This was her fifth time pressing the snooze button on her alarm clock. It felt like a betrayal that only a week after losing Blake, she had to lose Brady too. In an hour they would be driving Brady to the airport, where he would leave them for two years to teach the gospel and serve strangers like Jesus did when he was on the earth. Jordyn felt proud of him, but it hurt her, too, because it meant that she would now be the only child living at home. As if she needed another reason to feel lonely.

Jordyn hit the snooze button just one more time before rolling back over and closing her eyes effortlessly. She quickly fell asleep before the alarm sounded again.

"Jordyn."

Jordyn popped up under her covers—it wasn't just that she had heard her name, but that it had been Blake's voice saying it. She looked all around her room desperately searching, in hope that somehow, some way, Blake was there with her.

She knew it didn't make any sense to be disappointed, but the letdown of seeing her room completely empty came out in one single tear that fell down her right cheek. Would she someday not be able to remember how his voice sounded? What would she do if she couldn't remember every single detail about him anymore? The thought of that happening was debilitating to Jordyn. She instantly closed her eyes to picture everything she could about Blake—his blonde hair that swooped from his part to the left, the fact that he always wore shorts, even in the winter, his kind blue eyes, even his noticeable Adam's apple. She replayed his voice saying "Jordyn" in her head over and over again.

Kathleen knocked on Jordyn's bedroom door, bringing her back to the day's events. She slowly got out of bed. Jordyn knew she didn't have very long to get ready now, but she didn't feel like getting ready today, anyway. She grabbed the first shirt and pants that she found in the laundry basket of folded clothes she hadn't put away yet, and put them on. Jordyn's naturally wavy hair was perfect for a messy bun, so she did that to save on time.

Hurriedly grabbing her things, Jordyn went to unplug her phone and saw that she had a text from an unknown number.

Hey, Jordyn. I'm not sure you have my number, but it's Benson. I hope it's okay that I'm texting you.

Jordyn's heart sank as she walked over to her pushboard with the note that Blake had written to her and Benson. Jordyn read through the words that Blake wrote about Benson caring for her now and wondered if Benson knew about the note or not. She hardly even knew Benson. He had come over with Blake every so often, but she hadn't interacted with them much when he was there. All she knew about him now was that Blake must have trusted him to have left her in his care.

Jordyn had other demons to face right now with dropping Brady off at the airport. She definitely didn't have time to think of what to say to Benson, so she slid her phone into the back pocket of her blue jeans and went upstairs to leave with her family.

It was just her, Brady, and her parents. Jordyn's other brothers weren't able to make it this morning and had already said their goodbyes to Brady. After a few minutes of driving, Brady leaned over in the car and gently scratched Jordyn's back for the rest of the way to the airport. She was going to really miss his comforting presence. She had a feeling that she would really need it in these hard months and years to come. The problem with thinking about the future was that she could only see misery and darkness. Nothing could be fixed.

Their dad drove slowly into the parking garage, going up level after level. He finally pulled into a parking space that he found on level five. Brady stepped out of the car and put his backpack on his shoulders. Fred popped the trunk of the sedan open and lifted the suitcase out. Kathleen came around to Brady and adjusted his already perfectly straight tie one last time.

Brady and Jordyn let their parents walk ahead of them a little way, slowly trailing behind them.

They walked silently together for a minute before Brady whispered, "I'm going to miss you, favorite sister."

Jordyn choked up and couldn't reply. She leaned on him as they walked and nudged him teasingly as she often did. Brady pulled her into his side and they walked with arms around one another's backs.

"Make sure you write to me. I want to know how you're doing even though I'll be far away."

A little raspy, Jordyn replied, "I will."

They approached the security gate, where only Brady would pass through. Brady held their mom close and his strength now looked a lot like weakness as he started becoming emotional.

It was the first time Jordyn had seen him cry other than at the funeral. Still, Jordyn knew that his tears weren't weakness because through the tears, she could see courage in his eyes. Next, Jordyn's dad took his turn. Fred took advantage of every moment he could to teach his kids, and Jordyn saw him whisper something in Brady's ear as they embraced. She guessed that it was some sort of sage last-minute advice and encouragement for him.

Finally, Brady turned and looked at Jordyn. It only took that one look for Jordyn to lose control of her emotions. Brady pulled Jordyn into a tight hug. He let her fall apart in his arms yet again.

"You're going to need to stop doing that or I'm not going to be able to leave you here," Brady jokingly said, trying to soften the blow of his departure with humor.

With red eyes from crying with her, Brady looked steadily into Jordyn's eyes while grabbing her shoulders.

"We can do this."

Tears still streaming down, Jordyn slowly nodded to Brady.

"I need to hear you say it—we can do this," Brady insisted.

Jordyn swallowed and tried to wipe her eyes.

Hesitantly, she repeated slowly, "We . . . can . . . do . . . this."

Brady squeezed her shoulders and wiped away his own tears.

Brady needed to catch his plane, so the last goodbyes were quickly said. No one dared to prolong it anymore for fear of making it too hard for Brady to leave. Jordyn and her parents turned to exit, leaving Brady waiting in line to get through security. Jordyn almost made it without turning around to look at him, but suddenly she ran straight back to Brady in line to give him one last urgent embrace.

"Thank you for everything, Brady. I love you."

And that was it—just like that, he was on an airplane and Jordyn was alone with her parents. Jordyn sat very still in the back seat of the car all by herself, leaning on the door and looking out the window at the scenery passing by. She began to welcome the numb feeling that would come over her after the crying stopped. It felt better when her heart was so in shock that it allowed her a rest from feeling anything for a while.

Eventually, the car pulled into their driveway and each of them got out.

Fred spoke softly, "Hey, Jordyn—we bought some donuts and chocolate milk last night. I'm thinking we should eat some of these feelings away. What do you think?"

Fred always kept chocolate around for snacking, an activity in which Jordyn normally loved to join him.

With glazed eyes and her face drooping from heaviness, Jordyn responded, "I honestly just want to go lie down. Maybe later."

Fred seemed like he understood and even felt a little relieved, himself. He probably wasn't feeling very good either, and wouldn't have to keep up the facade of a positive attitude for the rest of the afternoon if Jordyn took a nap. They walked inside the house, where there was a chilliness that matched the family's mood perfectly.

Jordyn parted ways with her parents at the entryway, heading down the stairs as they went up the other flight. She found her favorite sweatpants to change into, and as she took her jeans off, her phone fell out of her back pocket. She remembered that she had never responded to Benson's text. She pulled her sweatpants on and picked her phone up off the floor before carrying it with her into Blake's room.

Gently, Jordyn slid down the brown quilt on his bed and

climbed in. She pulled the covers up to her chin with her phone still in her right hand.

Jordyn opened her phone and typed,

Hey Benson. Sorry it took so long for me to reply. How are you?

She hoped that was an okay reply since she wasn't quite sure what to say. Jordyn set her phone next to the pillow and rolled over, closing her eyes. She breathed in and held in Blake's scent as she started to doze. Right then, she heard a vibration coming from her phone. Could he be that quick at responding?

With nervous anticipation, Jordyn opened her eyes as she flipped open her phone.

It's all good! I actually just wanted to see how you are doing. I saw you across the lunchroom yesterday and knew I needed to find your number. I hope that's not creepy of me to ask someone for it.

When Jordyn read the text from Benson, a small smile emerged. His "creepy" comment reminded her of Blake and his humor. It made sense they'd have the same joking manner—they had been best friends, after all. She decided to continue the conversation with some humorous comment in return.

No, that's fine. It is a little creepy that you were staring at me across the lunchroom, though. ;)

After she sent the text to Benson, Jordyn realized that her text may have seemed like she was flirting with him. She wished she would have been able to take it back, but it was too late. It was too easy for her to joke with him since she felt like she was texting Blake. Before Benson could respond back to her text, Jordyn quickly turned her phone on silent mode so no one could reach her.

Jordyn rolled over onto her other side so her back was to her phone. It took a few minutes for her heart to stop pounding, but once it did, Jordyn escaped again into dreamland.

Chapter 6

Three weeks had passed since Blake's funeral and being at school had calmed down a little bit for Jordyn. Blake's suicide wasn't the hot topic anymore and people had moved on with their lives just as they had been before—everyone, that is, except for Jordyn. It was nice that she no longer got stopped in the halls and asked personal questions every five minutes, but it was still a nightmare for her to be at school.

Jordyn had no desire to catch up on the eight math assignments that she was now behind on, let alone to schedule a time with her teacher, Mrs. Randall, to take the test that had she missed for Blake's funeral. She knew she needed to take it eventually, but it reminded her of Blake since they were supposed to study for it together. She kept putting it off, even though Mrs. Randall would often ask her to stay after school to take it. Jordyn usually got home from school and went straight to bed. It was as if that was the only way she could get through the day. She supposed she could push her "nap appointment" back an hour after school, but that nap time was definitely more important to her than taking a test.

Math wasn't the only class that she was behind in. Jordyn was normally an A minus-type student, but she was earning about a

C average lately. Her teachers were trying to be understanding, but all they could do was allow her to turn in assignments late. They couldn't help much more if she wasn't doing her homework at all. Jordyn felt too overwhelmed with all the assignments she was late on, and didn't see any point in doing much of anything lately. Homework was at the bottom of her list of worries, and her list was pretty big.

It was time for Biology class to start and Jordyn purposely came in late to make sure Tessa didn't talk to her anymore. Tessa had trapped her a few more times since their first "talk" and Jordyn really couldn't stand being nice to her anymore. She liked this plan of ignoring Tessa better than the thought of yelling at her when she finally couldn't take it anymore.

Ms. Gregory always started class with a lecture, making it easy for Jordyn to slip away into her own thoughts. Jordyn stared out the window, watching the dripping rain hit the track that looped around the football field. She could still picture the day that Blake had wanted to try out for the track team and had begged her to come with him.

"I don't even enjoy running, Blake! That is the worst part of any sport and you are telling me that's what you want me to do with you *for* a sport?"

"Oh, come on. It will be fun. We will get to hang out together every day after school. I know you want to—deep down . . . . " Blake persisted.

"It must be super deep down, because I'm not finding it," Jordyn smirked back.

They both laughed before Jordyn rolled her eyes and gave in. She went to her room to change into shorts and a t-shirt before they left home. They got there five minutes late, and the team had already started doing drills around the track. From their parked van, they watched the runners doing drills that looked so silly and pointless to them.

"Maybe this wasn't such a good idea. I'd hate to look like that in front of everyone." Blake laughed as he admitted a change of heart, with Jordyn laughing right along with him.

Jordyn wished she could go back in time and sit in the van with him again and laugh easily, back when life was still okay.

She continued staring out the window at the wet track, thinking about how they went and got ice cream instead of trying out for the track team that day. It was one of those memories that made her stomach knot up inside, because it hurt to think that they were happy at one point. It wasn't fair that Blake had left her. She would be happy right now if he would have just stayed.

Jordyn suddenly noticed the student sitting behind her tapping her on the shoulder.

"Hey, the teacher is talking to you."

Jordyn's heart raced as she turned to see Ms. Gregory looking directly at her.

"We are taking out our books and turning to page 143," Ms. Gregory said kindly.

Even though the teacher wasn't angry with her, Jordyn still felt really embarrassed that everyone knew she wasn't paying attention in class. She put her blank note page away, pulled out her Biology book, and quickly turned to the correct page. Jordyn forced herself to keep her daydreaming in check so she didn't get called out again, at least for today.

When class ended, Jordyn quickly left her seat so she could get out before Tessa could talk to her. She was getting pretty good at making sure she was unreachable. Jordyn made her way from her locker toward the typical meeting spot at Livie's locker where she always met Livie, Sarah, and Ashley for lunch.

"I can't wait for Thanksgiving break! I'm so excited for school to be out for the rest of the week." Sarah skipped with enthusiasm as she talked.

"I'm most excited for this girl's sixteenth birthday party!!" Livie held Jordyn's hand before raising it up in the air triumphantly. Livie had planned a big birthday party for Jordyn at the roller skating rink downtown.

Greg came up behind them as they walked and stole Jordyn's hand from Livie's in the air and twirled her around.

"Well, if it isn't the birthday girl!" Greg dropped Jordyn's hand, but remained close to her. Jordyn felt tingles from where he had touched her hand.

Steve walked next to Greg and added, "And looking older—yet, not really wiser."

"Hey now. My birthday isn't until Friday." Jordyn blushed as she turned toward Greg. Their eyes met and Jordyn couldn't help but smile. She looked away, trying not to give away all she felt about him.

Greg thumped Steve on the chest and said, "Well, we will be there."

It had been such a long time since Jordyn had looked forward to anything. Maybe she would actually have some fun again. Were you supposed to have fun while you were grieving? Jordyn instantly got carried back into thoughts about Blake. She stayed quiet as the rest of the group changed the subject to their favorite Thanksgiving foods.

"The rolls dipped in gravy are definitely in the running," Ashley stated to the group.

"Oh, but rolls are even better with honey butter slathered all over them," Steve playfully disagreed.

Livie and Jordyn had started a secret poll at the beginning of the school year to guess when Steve would finally ask Ashley out on a date.

Livie turned to Jordyn and whispered, "I'm definitely going to win. He is going to ask her out before Christmas, I just know it."

Jordyn realized she had lost the thread of the conversation, but tried to jump back into a playful attitude by answering Livie, "Steve is way too reserved. Just you wait and see."

Jordyn grabbed her tray of food after paying at the register and followed the group to their usual table. She sat on the end in hopes she could stay out of most of the conversation so she could just be sad instead of trying to match their upbeat attitudes. Jordyn felt so stuck after losing Blake and it was difficult that her friends were moving on with normal life all around her. Jordyn ate a few bites of her taco and looked around the crowded lunchroom. Her eyes stopped when she saw Benson with his group of friends at a table across the room. They had texted back and forth a few times since his first text to her, but Jordyn still wasn't sure what to talk to him about. She kept looking at him and saw he was disengaged from his friends, too, his head hung low. Maybe she wasn't alone in missing Blake after all.

Benson looked up and saw Jordyn looking over at him. Jordyn didn't look away like she normally would. She looked him in the eyes and saw the hurt in his soul, just like she felt. She gave Benson a look of friendship and connection as she smiled slightly. Benson reciprocated, and even though it was comfortable making eye contact with him, she turned back toward her friends and listened again to their conversation.

Chapter 7

This weekend had been the very first family holiday since Blake's suicide, so it was difficult and draining for Jordyn's whole family. Her parents tried hard to make things the same as always, but the truth remained—nothing was the same. Turkey, her mom's famous rolls, and pumpkin pie could never distract Jordyn from the hole she had in her heart—a constant reminder of how miserable she was. The empty feeling in the house could be quickly measured by Brady and Blake's empty chairs surrounding Jordyn at the dinner table.

After helping her mom rinse the dishes from Thanksgiving dinner, Jordyn went downstairs into her room. Carefully, she thumbed through the stack of various papers and notepads in her desk cabinet and pulled out the blue bordered stationery paper. Jordyn sat staring blankly at the paper, unable to decide what to write.

Finally, she picked up the pen and wrote,

Dear Brady,

Jordyn froze again. How was she supposed to tell Brady anything when all she could think of was how much she hated everything? If she told him the truth, it would probably just leave him worried and upset. Jordyn's heart hurt even more when she thought about how he may be feeling today. Brady was more alone than she was, because he didn't have any family members with him at all. After another minute, Jordyn slid the letter to the side for later, right next to her stack of homework. She was really mastering procrastinating all the hard things.

Digging into the side pocket of her backpack, Jordyn searched for her earbuds and felt the cold metal of Blake's watch. She pulled both the headphones and watch out of her backpack and pressed the earbuds into each ear while she held the watch close to her chest. Jordyn went over to her bed and laid her head slowly back onto her pillow and closed her eyes as her music played. Slow and steady streams of tears flowed down Jordyn's cheeks until she dozed off to sleep.

* * *

The next morning, the curling iron was hot and Jordyn had already picked out a perfect outfit to wear skating—her favorite jeans and a light jacket that was cute and comfortable. She had always dreamed about turning sixteen years old. Her sweet sixteen wasn't as sweet as she had imagined it would be with Blake gone. This was the time in a girl's life to start figuring out who she is and who she wants to be, which is a lot to navigate all on its own without the added immutable hurt she felt from losing Blake. Her five older brothers used to tease her relentlessly about threatening all the boys who would want to date her. Jordyn had always hated the thought of what they might do to those poor boys, but now none of them were here to tease her and protect her from all the "evil" boys they warned her about. It definitely was anticlimactic compared to what she had pictured growing up.

Jordyn sat down in front of the small mirror on her dresser as she pinned up a section of her hair and began curling. She put the final touches on her makeup with some cream eyeshadow that highlighted her green eyes. Jordyn hoped that it would cover up the pain she could see in her eyes. With one last look in the mirror, she forced out a smile. Now she was ready for her birthday party.

* * *

The lights were dimmed low with spotlights swirling around the roller skating rink and music was blasting. Jordyn and Livie sat on a carpeted bench along the edge to put on their rental roller skates. As they were bent over tying them up, Ashley and Sarah surprised them as they rolled up from the other side of the rink.

"Hey, hey!" Ashley tried spinning in a circle on her skates but her left foot slid underneath her. Sarah tried to catch her but her efforts were in vain and they both fell clumsily onto their rear ends.

Sarah looked around to see if anyone else had noticed their incident and said, "This may be a long night for us."

All the girls giggled and Jordyn hoped she would look graceful tonight and not make a complete fool of herself by falling. She finished lacing up her skates and waited for Livie to take the lead and say that they were ready to start skating. Ashley and Sarah got up off the floor, and with arms hooked together, started skating away.

Ashley turned and yelled behind her, "We'll see you ladies out here soon, I hope!"

"I think I need a half-size bigger. These feel too tight on me." Livie got up from the bench and walked over to the skate rental counter. Jordyn watched Sarah lift one leg as she still held tight to Ashley's arm. She seemed like she was going to pull off her trick until a little boy skated right in front of them and caused them to change directions, leaving Sarah on the ground again. Ashley was still standing and laughed hysterically at Sarah until Sarah decided to pull Ashley down on the ground with her. Jordyn snickered to herself and turned to see how Livie was faring.

Livie was second in line now, and looked over at Jordyn with a bored expression. Jordyn returned her look with an encouraging thumbs-up. Just then, she noticed Greg and Steve walking in through the entrance. Greg was looking around as if he was searching for someone and Jordyn could feel the warmth in her cheeks when she realized that someone was likely her. As they walked further in, they saw Livie in line at the counter and started talking with her. Jordyn kept a close eye on them and suddenly Livie was pointing toward Jordyn and the bench. Before she could look away, Greg spotted her and smiled as he walked in her direction.

As Greg sat down on the bench, he reached over and gave Jordyn a hug.

"Happy birthday! I'm sorry we were running late. Steve apparently doesn't know how to tell time."

Jordyn smiled and responded, "We actually just got here too, so you're right on time."

"Good. I'm glad we haven't missed anything. I will be right back after I get my skates. I told Steve to wait in line for us but I'd better make sure he doesn't mess that up too."

Greg gently put his hand on the top of her left shoulder as he got up from the bench. As he walked away, Livie came back and sat next to her.

"I knew it was a good idea to invite Greg to your party," Livie teased as she slipped the first skate onto her foot.

"I am very grateful for your thoughtfulness." Jordyn giggled.

As they both laughed, Jordyn looked up and made eye contact with Greg in line. Jordyn was ecstatic she was finally old enough to date according to her family rules and hoped that Greg really did like her back. She had always felt a special connection between them as their friendship had grown over the years.

"Let's do this," Livie announced as she stood up with her skates tied.

Jordyn got up off the bench and wobbled a little bit as she put one foot in front of the other.

As she began to balance herself out and started to trust that she was in control, Ashley and Sarah came from behind her—Ashley on her left side, and Sarah on her right. They each grabbed an arm and launched Jordyn forward. After the speed from the boost forward wore off, the three girls caught up with Jordyn.

Sarah snickered as she said, "We love you, Jordyn!"

Ashley sped away from the group with Sarah following right behind. Being with Sarah and Ashley was always a fun time because they were constantly being crazy and enjoying life, but lately, Jordyn didn't like to be around them as much. Her life was much more serious ever since Blake's suicide; she didn't really fit into their fun-filled and light-hearted world now.

After a few times of skating around the rink together, Livie turned to Jordyn and yelled out, "Don't look now, but someone is headed your way!"

Unable to resist looking, Jordyn turned to see Greg and Steve making their way across the middle of the rink to catch up with them.

As the boys approached them, Jordyn called out to Greg, "You look pretty skilled at skating with weaving through all those people to get here."

Greg continued the banter with, "Just showing my determination to get to you as fast as I could."

The loud music stopped and a man's voice came on the intercom saying, "All ladies line up around the skating rink. It's time for boys' choice."

Livie and Jordyn skated to the side and found Ashley and Sarah already standing on the edge of the rink, ready to be chosen. The slow music began and Steve was quick to hold out his hand to Ashley as they skated off together, hand in hand.

"See, I told you—I'm going to win the bet." Livie looked proud to have made her guess sooner than Jordyn, and for the first time, Jordyn thought Livie just might be right.

Jordyn tried not to look too disappointed when Greg skated off and around the rink. She wished he would have asked her to skate right away like Steve did. Her heart dropped as she thought he might not pick her after all, so she decided to talk to Livie instead of watching for Greg to come back around—just in case. Before any words came out, Jordyn heard someone clear their throat. She turned in relief to see Greg holding his hand out for her to skate with him.

"Wow! Your hand is freezing. It's lucky that I came along to help you out!" Greg looked over at Jordyn and his eyes pierced through the shield around her that she worked so hard to keep up. Every time Greg looked at her, Jordyn couldn't help but melt inside a little more— and now he would surely see it.

Trying to sound more confident than she felt, Jordyn responded, "You are truly my hero."

"That's a pretty important position to have, but I'm up for the task!" Greg held Jordyn's hand a little tighter.

"Can I ask you something, Jordyn?" Greg sounded serious.

Jordyn, a little worried, replied, "Sure."

"I hope this isn't too soon, but I would love to take you on a real date if that's okay."

Jordyn was shocked that he had asked her out already. Her heart started pounding and she hoped Greg wasn't able to hear it. "I would love that."

Although they were silent as they skated now, Jordyn felt comfortable. She was soaking in every moment of the slow song but could tell it was about to end.

Right then, the same little boy who sped in front of her friends earlier went right in front of her and Greg and they tripped as they swerved out of the way. Somehow Greg landed on the floor and caught Jordyn in his arm.

"And I saved you again!" Greg helped her up and tucked the stray hair behind her ear.

A little embarrassed but mostly relaxed, Jordyn responded, "What would I ever do without you?"

Greg escorted Jordyn off the skating rink to the trusty carpet bench so they could recover from their fall. Jordyn adjusted her jacket and brushed off some dust from her pant leg.

Greg got serious again and asked, "So, how are you doing?"

Jordyn knew what he really was asking. He was really wanting to know if she was dealing with Blake's death and how she was dealing with it. It was an extremely loaded question with a very loaded answer—an answer that Jordyn wasn't sure she was ready to give, and not sure that Greg would even be ready to hear.

"I'm okay."

Jordyn thought about her answer—what did 'okay' even mean? It sounded vague enough, so she was going with it.

"But really, Jordyn. I can't even believe what you must be going through."

Greg's words cut deep and Jordyn again felt isolated. He *didn't* know what she was going through. No one seemed to understand how she was doing.

With a bleak face, all she could say was, "Honestly, I can't either."

Reality couldn't even escape Jordyn on her special day. One thought about Blake's suicide changed her whole mood and she couldn't believe she had let herself enjoy the party. She couldn't be normal or date or even just hang out with friends normally. There was no way to really be happy anymore.

Jordyn untied her skates and returned them at the counter. Greg sat beside her as she waited for her ride home. She thanked him for saving her as she left, but what she really needing saving from was too much for anyone.

Chapter 8

J ordyn sat in between her parents on the church bench the
following Sunday morning. She had stayed up late into
the night looking through photos of Blake, so nine in the
morning had come way too early for her. Not wanting to be
alert, Jordyn rested her head on Fred's shoulder. Because she
was the youngest and the only daughter in the family, she had
always been his baby girl and he had a huge soft spot for her.
In his eyes, she could do no wrong.

The organ music bellowed as the congregation joined in
singing hymns. Jordyn remained nestled against her father
with her eyes closed since she couldn't muster up even one
ounce of desire to sing praises with everyone else. The music
only made her sleepier and as the sounds surrounding her faded,
Jordyn began to fade as well.

"Oh, sweetie." Fred gently nudged Jordyn to wake up.

As Jordyn was coming to her senses, she could see the
congregation leaving and hear the loud chatter. She quietly
bent over and grabbed her scripture bag and purse from under
the bench. It was now time for class with her friends. She used
to share and talk a lot in class, but lately she was more of a quiet
observer who made her way to the chair in the very back. All of
the teenagers were talking to each other and laughing as they

walked to Sunday School. The girls would always sit on one side of the room while the boys sat on the other. Ashley and Sarah didn't let that stop them, though, as they had their own conversation going across the room with Steve and his friend Tyson.

"Okay, okay. Quiet down, everyone."

Edwin Ross walked into the classroom and closed the door. Edwin was twenty-four years old and had been living at home to save money while he finished his Master's degree. He was almost as tall as the top of the doorway, and had a handsome half-smile that some of the girls in the class swooned over.

"Here we go with the usual. Go around and tell us one fun thing that you did this past weekend. I'll start. I stuffed myself so full with turkey and stuffing that I could hardly even move for the rest of the day. It was fantastic."

The boys went first, and when Greg's turn came, he said, "My favorite part of this weekend was Jordyn's birthday party."

Immediately the rest of the class teased, "Ooooh!"

Jordyn covered her red face with her scarf and hoped the embarrassment would go away once Steve started talking.

Steve agreed, "I would have to say that Jordyn's birthday was also my favorite!"

On cue, the rest of the class did their part with another whooping "Ooooh!"

This time though, it had Jordyn smiling as well. It was the perfect way to take the attention off of her and Greg—although, Jordyn secretly liked that there was enough there to be teased over.

"Okay. Your turn, Jordyn. I'm guessing your favorite part about this weekend was *also* your birthday party?"

Jordyn was grateful that her teacher gave her the escape from having to talk today and she just nodded in agreement. Now she could fade away in the back of the class, just like she had done for the past month. It was hard for her to stay focused during church. She had way too much time to idly think. Thoughts came to her from before Blake died and what she could have done differently to prevent it, along with thoughts of how she would ever face the rest of her life without him. She felt as if she would live the rest of her life being hollow inside.

Jordyn shut her eyes and let down the wall she tried to keep up, letting all of the misery crash over her that she was continuously attempting to fight off. Then she glanced around the room to see smiles and bright eyes on the faces of her peers. It wasn't fair that no one else had to deal with this. Another weight of misery dropped from her chest to her stomach. She couldn't imagine possibly feeling any heavier, but apparently she was wrong.

"Jordyn."

She looked up to see that Edwin was about to ask her something.

"When was a time in your life that you exercised faith?"

Panic took over Jordyn in a way that it never had before. She wasn't capable of answering a question about faith when she didn't believe it could help her anymore. She couldn't think of an answer just to please her teacher and classmates enough that they would move on with the lesson in a pleasant way. She couldn't pretend that much.

Without a second thought, Jordyn stood up from her chair and hurried to the door. She turned the handle of the brown door and ran quickly into the women's bathroom. She hurried across the tile floor and shut herself into the furthest stall from the entrance. This may be a different bathroom than Debra's, but it was the same desperate escape she had felt that dreadful Friday afternoon. As she double-checked to make sure the stall was locked, she hit her fist against the door. Grabbing her sore hand, she melted down the brick wall and onto the floor. Jordyn brought her fisted hand up to her mouth to hold in her sobs. Whether she wanted to or not, nothing—not even faith—could keep her from feeling all of the agony that was inside of her. It was a part of who she was now.

Knowing that Livie would come looking for her eventually, she forced herself up and decided she could hide out in her dad's car until the church services were over. She couldn't face anyone, especially now. She hurried out the back door of the church and walked toward where they had parked earlier near the back east corner. There was a cold breeze that had been blowing all day long, but at least it was sunny out, so the car would be warm enough. Jordyn wrapped her sweater around her waist and climbed inside the unlocked door to the back seat.

Her parents seemed to look forward to coming to church, but Jordyn hated how she felt when she was there. Every bit of her soul ached while she was inside those doors, and she was glad to be out. She knew her parents would be disappointed if they found out she had left her class, but she felt too much relief to care. Now she could be as miserable as she wanted to without any thought of worry.

Jordyn attempted to breathe out all the anxiety from her body and closed her eyes again. She rested her head against the cold window. The slight chill didn't bother her, but actually helped awaken her senses. Jordyn sat silently while the rivers of sorrow flowed down from the corners of her eyes, down her cheeks, and even across her lips until she felt the empty numb feeling start to take over her body.

She watched listlessly out the back window when she noticed that some people were starting to exit the church. She still didn't want to see or talk to anyone, so she decided she would just wait in the car until her parents came outside. She realized it wasn't a great plan, but it was the only one she had.

Almost fifteen minutes passed by with no sign of her parents. It was odd that they weren't out yet, but she couldn't risk coming out of the car even now with the parking lot almost empty. She decided to stick to her plan and to just close her eyes and wait it out.

Jordyn hadn't realized she'd dozed off until she heard the slam of the front car doors as her parents climbed in and buckled their seatbelts.

"You must be freezing out here, Jordyn! Why didn't you wait for us inside? Did you not remember that we were meeting with Bishop Johnson right after?" Kathleen was always so concerned about keeping her kids warm outside. It didn't matter how old they got, she always asked them if they had a jacket or a coat on every single time they were about to leave the house.

Jordyn avoided looking at Kathleen before replying honestly, "Oh, nope. I didn't remember you mentioning that. It's okay though. I was just fine out here."

Jordyn realized her hands were actually really cold, but she didn't want her parents to know that she had been outside in the car for over an hour now.

"Oh, yeah." Fred remembered, turning toward the back seat, "Here you go, Jordyn. You must have left these behind in class."

Jordyn's heart stopped when she saw her dad handing the maroon scripture bag over his head toward her. Did they know she had skipped out on class today? Did someone tell them how she left class and never came back? Jordyn was never one for lying, but she didn't feel like she could talk to her parents openly about everything she was going through. It was hard enough feeling the way she did, but it would be even more difficult to swallow if she was disappointing them and causing them to worry. Jordyn just hoped they didn't know she was lying to them.

"Thanks." She took her scriptures without further comment.

Jordyn was relieved when her parents didn't bring anything else up. She was saved—at least this time.

Chapter 9

Tuesday. Jordyn had a new theory about waking up in the morning. She was pretty sure that her broken heart wasn't able to pump enough blood through her body to give her enough energy for a whole day, so she had to sleep extra long to make up for it. It was becoming a fierce battle every single morning to wake up and go to school. Most of the mornings lately involved her pushing snooze repeatedly or not waking up to her alarm at all until Kathleen finally knocked on the door telling her she had to get up. Then Jordyn would throw some clothes on and attempt to fix her messy hair before eating the breakfast Kathleen brought for her as she drove Jordyn to school.

Yesterday, all of her friends had played off her leaving in the middle of Sunday School the day before, acting as if nothing had happened. Part of her was grateful that she didn't have to talk about things with anyone, but part of her felt even more empty and alone than before. With every day that went by, she felt like she had less and less in common with her friends.

As Jordyn was walking to her first class, she was startled by someone grabbing her shoulder from behind.

"I'm so glad I found you. Have you heard?"

It was Benson, which was a little strange to her since they

had only talked through texting before now.

When she finished processing, she opened her mouth. "Have I heard what?"

Benson motioned her to the side of the hallway and spoke softly, "Another student died by suicide last night."

Immediately, Jordyn's throat seemed to swell shut and the memories and senses of the day she had lost Blake rushed through her. She felt a sharp pain in her chest and her body was frozen.

"I knew I had to find you and tell you before you heard it through the school announcements."

Still frozen, Jordyn heard Benson speaking, but wasn't able to respond. The tardy bell rang and Benson gently guided her arm through his and helped her walk outside.

"Do you want to take a drive with me?"

Jordyn looked at Benson and nodded. He led her to his Ford F-150, opened the passenger door, and held Jordyn's hand as she stepped up and into the truck. As soon as Jordyn sat down onto the faux leather seats, her head collapsed into her lap and she wept uncontrollably.

Benson got into the driver's seat and brushed Jordyn's hair to one side to rub her back as he allowed her to fall apart. Almost naturally, Jordyn leaned over and laid her head on his right leg as she continued to cry. Even though she didn't enjoy crying in front of anyone, she felt safe with Benson. He seemed to genuinely care about her and she knew he was dealing with the loss of her brother too. She finally felt free to show her emotions because she knew that Benson was capable of handling her feelings and wouldn't be shocked by them.

After a minute, Benson turned the key and the engine sputtered for a moment before it purred. Jordyn sat up and used her sleeve to wipe her face.

"Oh, sorry, Jordyn. You don't need to sit up. I was just turning the heater on for you."

She hadn't even noticed how cold she was until he said that.

"Thank you." Jordyn looked over at Benson and gave him a brief smile before turning away toward her window.

"I just can't believe it. I feel everything all over again and I didn't know it was even possible. Even now I am barely even functioning day-to-day. I miss Blake so much."

Benson's voice was slow and steady. "I do too, Jordyn."

His attentiveness gave Jordyn the confidence to confide in him. She faced toward Benson again. "The truth is, I can't escape him. That seems bad to say because I obviously want to remember him, but everywhere I turn, he left a mark. My house is full of him. The school is full of him. My church is full of him. How dare he leave that burden on me! How dare he leave me!"

This was the first time Jordyn had vocalized these thoughts and even though it hurt, there was a tiny bit of relief that came with it too.

"He loved you. You know that, right? Every time you came up in conversation, he was the proudest brother. I know that you were a happy spot in his life. " Benson looked compassionate, but spoke in a firm tone.

Jordyn's tear ducts never seemed to dry up. "I wish that was enough for him to stay."

"None of this is on you, Jordyn. That's not fair to do to yourself."

"Nothing about this is fair, Benson. I'm so tired of feeling this way." Jordyn said with a voice that was clearly defeated.

Benson rubbed Jordyn's back again as she hunched over with

her hands covering her face. Their silence was just confirmation to Jordyn that there was nothing that could be done or said done or said to fix the awful mess that was now her life.

Jordyn could have sat like that forever, but finally lifted her head up.

"I apologize that you had to see all of this. It's not a pretty sight."

She pulled the sun visor down and opened the cover to the mirror. As she wiped the black around her eyes, Benson comforted her with, "You look great, I promise."

Jordyn turned to him with rosy cheeks and suggested, "I think I'm ready for that drive now."

While she reached across her body for the seatbelt, she could see in the corner of her eye that Benson was smiling shyly. Jordyn had never noticed the slight dimple in his right cheek before. All he had ever been before was Blake's friend, but now she was seeing him in a whole new way.

Benson reached into his pocket and took out a quarter. "Here. Flip a coin to see what direction we go. Heads we go right, and tails we go left."

"It sounds like too much adventure for me, but okay."

Jordyn held her left hand to the side and Benson placed the coin on her palm. She gently put the quarter on her thumb and flipped it up into the air. To the surprise of both—and to Jordyn's terror—the quarter didn't aim the way she had hoped and instead catapulted right into Benson's eye.

"Oh my goodness! Benson! I'm so sorry. Are you alright?"

As he squeezed his left eye closed, he teased, "I just may need you to buy me a parrot to match the eye patch I'll need to wear from here on out!"

Jordyn couldn't help but chuckle. "I'll get right on that for you."

With a continued sense of confidence from their interactions, she cleared her throat and quickly stated, "Blake left me a note about you, asking you to take care of me."

The silence that followed made her regret opening her mouth and it confirmed to her that he hadn't known about Blake's note. She thought he must have known; it explained why he originally reached out to her after Blake's death.

After a sustained pause, Benson asked, "What do you mean, Blake left a note for you about me?"

"I found a note in his room where he wrote that you were supposed to take care of me now, and even tease me. I thought you knew. I was shocked to find it, especially since you and I had never talked before. I can't believe he planned and thought about someone taking care of me."

"I do, Jordyn. You meant so much to him. He wouldn't even let me talk about how cute I think you are, so I'm a little surprised that he would have picked me."

Jordyn's eyes widened as her cheeks warmly reddened. "I never knew that."

They both sat still for a minute until Jordyn finally picked the quarter up off of the car mat.

"It looks like we're supposed to go left." She tilted the coin toward Benson and showed him that the tails side had landed up.

Benson's dimple showed again as he flashed a charming smile Jordyn's way. They drove around the back roads of town together until lunchtime.

Chapter 10

Kathleen cleared her throat after finishing the rice on her plate. It had been quiet since they had started eating dinner, so Jordyn looked up toward Kathleen at the silence being disrupted.

"Your father and I would like to talk to you."

Nothing about that statement sounded promising. Jordyn's heart rate sped up and she knew that she was in for trouble at Kathleen's tone of voice.

"We are really concerned. I received a phone call from your Vice Principal that you've skipped school and you're failing three of your classes."

Kathleen paused to let her respond, but Jordyn didn't have anything to say.

Jordyn could see the fear in her mother's eyes as they started to well up. There was no way that she could face looking over at her dad to see the disappointment and distress she was causing him. She wished that she could put on a fake smile for them and seem like she had things together, but she was too exhausted to even try.

"We also told your boss up at the school that you won't be working until further notice. They can't keep your job open if you're not going to be there."

Jordyn looked up at this. It wasn't like her parents to let her just quit.

"We have made an appointment with a therapist for tonight at 7:30. Also, we will need to talk with all of your teachers and see how we can get you caught up in your classes. The Vice Principal has let your teachers know that we are going to be making a plan with them."

Still, silence was the only response Jordyn could offer.

Fred quietly gestured, "We just love you and want to help. We're here for you always."

Even though she knew that was true, it would hurt everyone more if she was honest with them. She glanced out of the corner of her eye to Fred and quickly looked away when she saw the beginnings of pain she knew would be written all over his face.

More out of desperation to be done with this uncomfortable conversation than courage, Jordyn cleared her throat and spoke up.

"Can I be excused now?"

Kathleen looked doubtful. "But we just wanted to . . . "

Kathleen was interrupted by Fred placing his arm on hers as he answered Jordyn with a gentle, "Sure, sweetie."

Jordyn didn't hesitate to stand up, putting her plate in the kitchen sink and hurrying downstairs to her room. She quickly closed her door but prevented it from slamming behind her, and collapsed into her bed. All of these difficulties she was required to handle were too much and she didn't know how to start digging herself out. One thing was for sure though—she did not want to talk to a random stranger about all of it. How could they sign her up for therapy without even discussing it with her first? She understood it must be hard for her parents to watch her struggle, but this was not helping her one bit.

As she squeezed her pillow as tight as she could against her chest, she saw out of the corner of her eye the unfinished letter to Brady on the side of her desk. *Maybe it's time to tell Brady what a disappointment I am, too. I wouldn't want to leave him out!* She thought bitterly.

Jordyn walked over to her desk and with determination, pulled out her favorite pen again to start writing.

I hate being the only child living at home. I hate not being able to sleep in. I hate not being able to do whatever I want. I hate sitting in church feeling like everyone is looking at me and judging me. I hate people telling me what to do, and what I need to change. I hate that I think my friends are talking about me behind my back. I hate the feeling that no one understands how I feel so alone, and whenever I start to feel happy, I feel guilty because Blake is gone. I hate that our brother is dead, and the way he went. I hate the very thought of suicide. I hate how I'm messed up and have depression now because of his death. I hate visiting Blake at a grave. I hate the fear of not being able to trust someone, and that they'll be gone someday. I hate to see people hurt. I hate when I hurt someone. I hate that I'm not stronger in the gospel. I hate that my life is falling apart. I hate that my testimony is dwindling. I hate how I'm afraid to get close to anyone. I hate how I'm making a hate list instead of being grateful.

Jordyn took a moment to reread her soul-splattered letter and with every sentence, the pit in her stomach grew and grew. She knew that there was no way she could send this to Brady, but she couldn't lie to him either, and anything but this letter to him would be a lie. Jordyn crumpled it into a ball and shot it into her miniature trash can across the room.

There never seemed to be a good time to tell the truth of what she was going through. It was like it was a secret she had to hide within herself forever, and now in a few hours, her parents were going to try and fix her at therapy. There was nothing that could be done to fix anything. Unless this therapist had magic powers to go back in time, Jordyn could see no possible way that this was going to help.

* * *

When they walked into the door of the family therapist's office, Jordyn's first impression was how dark it was in there because of the privacy blinds on every window. She realized it made sense to have so much privacy, but a more inviting space would be appreciated since she already was wary about coming. The receptionist gave each of them a hand-held tablet to answer questions about how they had been feeling in the past week along with a rating scale of zero to ten to answer with.

As Jordyn sat in her green armchair, she read the first question: "How would you rate your mood this past week (zero being completely miserable and ten being ecstatic about life)?"

Jordyn's first thought was that there was no way anyone who answered this first question as a ten would even be here at therapy. Then, as her heart answered zero, she tapped a four. She knew that this was supposed to be confidential, but if there was any chance that her parents saw this, they would be worried sick with her real answer. She quietly answered the remainder of the questions in the same way.

Jordyn looked up when she heard the mysterious door to the back begin to open. In the doorway, a man dressed in business casual stood and stated, "I'm ready for the Alden family."

Jordyn never realized that it was a group therapy session with her *and* her parents. She watched as her parents got up from their matching armchairs and walked toward the man at the door. Her legs felt heavy as she finally stood up to follow behind. The heaviness she felt must be her body's way of trying to save her from the agonizing situation that was surely beyond that door.

To Jordyn's surprise, her heavy legs did move forward even though she wished they wouldn't. Her stomach was uneasy and she could feel her heart pounding. At the end of the long narrow hallway, the man led them into a small office. There was a couch where her parents sat, a loveseat where she sat, and the man sat beside a desk in an office chair on wheels.

"My name is Cory. It's really nice to meet you all. I realize that I'm a stranger to you, so I'd like to take a minute to tell you a bit about myself before we get started."

As Cory spoke about his passion for rock climbing and camping, Jordyn's mind was too full of worry to follow what he was saying. Fred went next and introduced their family to Cory. Jordyn's ears tuned in again when she heard him say "Blake."

"Is that your son who took his life?" Cory questioned while writing notes on a sheet of paper inside a folder.

As Fred and Cory spoke back and forth, Jordyn sat completely still while staring straight forward at the blank white wall. Kathleen occasionally spoke up when Cory spoke to her directly, but she didn't seem to be as comfortable as Fred was with speaking openly about their life. Jordyn may have been okay sharing some things with Cory, but not in front of her parents.

Just as she thought she might get away with not talking at all, Cory directed his first question at her.

"Jordyn, would you tell me a little bit about how you've been feeling since your brother died?"

She wished she could just disappear. She kept staring forward and answered, "I'm okay."

Before Cory even had time to respond to her, Kathleen spoke up, "Jordyn, you are not okay."

Cory sat back for a moment to see what would happen. Jordyn held firm and remained silent. This made Kathleen even more irritated and you could hear it in her voice when she said, "You need to say something, Jordyn!"

"I don't want to talk about it, Mom!" This was the first time Jordyn had raised her voice to her parents, and she knew that it was wrong to do so, but she couldn't get out of this situation without doing it. There was no way around it.

Luckily, Cory stepped in and directed more questions toward her parents for the last five minutes of their session. Relieved, Jordyn took a deep breath in and closed her eyes while they talked. She remained quiet during the whole car ride home.

As soon as she walked into their house, Jordyn ran downstairs and pulled her phone out. She found Benson's name and sent him a text.

Meet me tomorrow during first period?

After receiving a thumbs-up emoji back from Benson, she lay down and went to sleep so she could get tonight as far away from her as possible.

Chapter 11

Things were a little tense the next morning between Jordyn and her mother. Jordyn could tell by the look in her eyes that Kathleen had a million things to say, but luckily for Jordyn, she let her go with only, "I hope you have a good day today and get caught up on a few things with your teachers."

Jordyn felt like a packed sardine walking through the main hallway to her locker. Her high school was the largest school in the area and it wasn't unusual to not know any of the other students surrounding you. In a clearing through the continuous flow of people, Jordyn saw Greg standing in front of her locker. He was scanning the surroundings waiting for her. When their eyes met, Jordyn couldn't help but smile pleasantly.

In a panicky voice, Greg blurted out,

"I tried looking for you yesterday. I wanted to make sure that you were okay after I heard the announcements."

Greg's eyes were sincere and concern seemed to radiate out of him. It made Jordyn feel guilty that she had been with Benson and wasn't around when Greg was looking for her.

"I hope you're okay," Greg continued.

"You are the absolute sweetest, Greg. It was really hard and I left for a little bit with a friend, so that's probably why you couldn't find me."

Greg pulled Jordyn in for a hug and gently said, "Well, at least I found you now."

Jordyn felt secure in his arms. He was warm and she could smell his cologne as she took a deep breath in. For a brief moment, everything around her seemed to dissipate and there could have been a million students around them and she wouldn't have cared. In an effort to not linger too long, Greg gave Jordyn a tight squeeze and then released his arms slowly from around her.

"When you're ready, let me walk you to class at the Seminary Building." Greg had been raised like a gentleman, and he was very good at being one.

"That would be great, but I am actually meeting my friend again instead of going to Seminary—because I really need to talk to someone."

Jordyn could see the disappointment surface in Greg's face. He probably understood her need to talk with someone, but it wasn't with him *and* it was during Seminary when she would have had the chance to be spiritually uplifted. She knew how important Seminary attendance was to Greg—it had been important to Jordyn before losing Blake—but it hadn't proved to be very helpful lately.

"You know that I'm always here for you too, right?" Greg's eyes had that same goodness and concern as when he had first started talking with her, even through his disappointment at her skipping Seminary.

"Of course I know you are. Thank you. You are always so great to me."

Jordyn closed her locker and put her arm through his and encouraged, "How about I walk you to *your* first class?" She locked her eyes with his to make sure that he knew how much she appreciated him in her life.

Jordyn realized how nice it was to walk, carefree on Greg's arm for a few minutes. *This is what I would be experiencing all of the time if her world hadn't been turned upside down by Blake's suicide.* She pushed that thought out of her mind and turned her attention back to Greg. She loved how excellent he was at showing her that he cared about her and she was hoping that he would make specific plans soon for going on their date together. It was the one thing that she had to look forward to in her life right now.

They soon arrived at Greg's classroom, to Jordyn's dismay. She wished they could spend the whole day together. As Jordyn was turning to leave after saying her final goodbye to him, Greg grabbed her hand and guided her back to face him.

"I want to spend more time with you."

Jordyn realized that Greg was still holding onto her hand and she felt the butterflies flutter full-swing inside her stomach.

"I suppose I can stay for a few more minutes," she replied flirtatiously.

Greg's tall-dark-and-handsome features were accentuated when he smiled. "I'm glad it's agreed upon. Now, how do you feel about Chinese food?"

Jordyn raised her eyebrow and asked, "Why do you want to know?" She hoped that this was leading exactly where she wanted it to.

"Oh, no reason. Just curious about your eating habits."

"Yeah, I'm sure that's it. I suppose that I'll be nice and play along. I have all positive feelings towards Chinese food. It has never led me astray."

Greg gently released his hand from hers and fished through

71

his backpack until he pulled out a notebook. Jordyn watched as he turned to a blank page and began to write.

"What in the world are you doing?" she giggled.

Jordyn was unable to contain her laughter as she watched Greg jot down notes with the determination of any good detective.

"I'm the one asking questions around here, young lady," Greg teasingly corrected her.

He continued, "And what is your favorite winter time activity?"

Jordyn furrowed her eyebrows again at Greg, and right as she started to open her mouth with a clever comeback, she felt a tap on her shoulder. She turned around and was surprised to see Benson looking back at her. Benson spoke before she could.

"Sorry I keep startling you from behind. It's a nasty habit that I'm trying to break."

Jordyn was unsure how to handle this situation. If Greg found out that Benson was the one that she was skipping class with, she wasn't sure how he would take it.

"Oh, that's okay. Greg, this is Benson. He was one of Blake's friends."

Greg looked relieved to hear that Benson was Blake's friend, and certainly not a threat to him. However, his look quickly changed as soon as Benson opened his mouth again to speak.

"Hey there! Nice to meet you. Are you ready to go, Jordyn?"

Jordyn tried to ease Greg's mind. "Uh, yes. Greg, would you be alright if we finish this interrogation later?" She touched his forearm reassuringly, giving him a smile. Greg nodded in agreement, but Jordyn could see that she left him feeling discouraged again as he didn't hide his emotions very well.

She hated feeling like she had hurt him, especially because it seemed to be a common theme in her life lately—disappointing the people she cared about.

That's why she liked talking to Benson so much—she felt like she could never disappoint him. He treated her in a way that made it possible to be vulnerable, and she knew he shared this hurt with her. It was easy to be with him because she didn't need to be anything more than the way she was feeling at that particular moment. As they walked out to his truck, her shoulders began to loosen and she took a deep breath of the crisp winter air as the snow crunched under her feet.

Like last time, Jordyn was able to pour out her thoughts and feelings to Benson. He let her vent about how her parents had ambushed her and how she couldn't tell them what she was going through. She cried and he comforted her. He listened to her and they joked and laughed together. Jordyn felt good for once and she didn't regret it, even though she knew it came with a cost. She was sure that her mom would find out about her skipping class again, but to feel good was a good enough reason for her.

First period was almost over, so Benson started driving toward the school instead of the endless random circles they had been driving around for the past hour.

"Maybe next time we hang out, we could do it other than in the middle of school and without getting ourselves in trouble," Jordyn suggested.

"Now, what's the fun in that?" Benson asked conspiratorially.

Jordyn turned toward Benson, and for the first time, realized that he seemed to be okay with missing school. She started to wonder if he did this often, or if he and Blake had ever gotten in trouble missing school together before. Jordyn dug a little deeper.

"Maybe it would be fun *not* getting into trouble, though. Does your mom not get mad at you like mine does?"

Benson looked confident as he replied.

"I have a whole system worked out. Both of my parents work, so I just delete the messages before either of them gets home. It's really no big deal. My parents are way too busy to notice anything that I'm doing, so I get away with pretty much anything I want to."

Jordyn was surprised by this. Even though it seemed nice to be able to get away with some things, it made her somewhat concerned that Benson may not be the kind of boy she wanted to be hanging out with. Her parents definitely wouldn't have approved of all of the times Blake had gone over to Benson's house after school without any parents there. On the other hand, Benson had been extremely nice to her and had been the one person that she had been able to fully open up to for months now. She couldn't lose that. Not now.

"On that note, I was going to invite you to a party at my house next weekend. A little bit of fun could be just what the doctor ordered."

Jordyn was hesitant and unsure of how to feel about all of this. Benson seemed like a great guy, but something in her felt uneasy.

"My parents would never let me. I'm pretty sure my mom would rather I catch up on homework, as a matter of fact."

They pulled into the school parking lot and Benson parked the truck in one of the only empty parking spots near the back. Benson turned toward Jordyn with his dimpled grin.

"That's why you don't tell her. Or you could just tell them that you've been invited to hang out with some of Blake's friends.

That's the harmless truth, isn't it? They might not mind if they thought it'd cheer you up."

Jordyn unbuckled her seatbelt and hopped down out of the truck. The bulky door slammed shut even with her gentle push. She walked around the extended bed of the truck and met back up with Benson to walk into the school building. They were right on time and merged into the students that were walking back to the school from the Seminary building.

"Hmmm, maybe. I'll have to think about it, okay?" They stopped as they reached Jordyn's locker.

"Sounds like a deal, but I have a feeling that you'll see things my way."

Benson went in to give Jordyn a hug. She felt her heart thudding in her chest and her nervousness grew. The hug lasted a short moment, but Benson stayed close enough to look down at her and clear away a stray hair by softly stroking his finger across her forehead. Benson smiled at her as he walked backwards to part ways. He stayed facing toward her, still staring at her. Jordyn was growing fond of seeing that dimple come out whenever he smiled at her. Benson eventually bumped into someone since he wasn't looking where he was going, but quickly caught himself. They both laughed and he eventually turned away to go to his next class.

"Ahem. Who was that?" Jordyn nearly dropped her book as she closed her locker door to reveal Livie standing there.

"Oh," Jordyn tried to sound casual, "that was just Blake's friend, Benson." She hoped that this answer would satisfy Livie enough to drop the subject.

"Uh-huh. He looked like he was quite *friendly* with you, actually." Livie teased and fluttered her eyelashes at Jordyn.

"That is not funny, Livie. He is just a friend of Blake's, who is now my friend."

Livie tilted her head in an expression stating her disbelief.

"We are just friends. Just. Friends." Jordyn emphasized.

Livie shrugged skeptically, but started talking about her plans for Christmas break, which was coming up in a couple of days. Jordyn was so grateful to have the change of topic. She wondered privately to herself, though, if maybe Greg *should* be worried about Benson after all.

Chapter 12

It was Christmas break and Jordyn could finally forget about school for two weeks. She was sure that her mother would not forget, but she could most definitely, absolutely, positively forget. It made Jordyn nervous that she would have so much free time on her hands, but it was nice to be able to relax from the extra stress that school put on her. It wasn't only the classes and homework that stressed her out, but also the roller coaster of emotions she felt each day at the school she had once shared with Blake, and trying to act normally despite all that. There was nothing that could have prepared her for this kind of tragedy in her life, and she couldn't easily steer through the stormy water that was her day-to-day life. Jordyn was still feeling disconnected from the world, so it was going to be a breath of fresh air to be able to stay home and be alone.

Saturday came and went. Jordyn had planned to even clean her room that day, but sleeping in and lounging around was quite time-consuming, leaving no space for any other activities. Sunday morning rolled around and it was time to start waking up to get ready for church. Jordyn was overtaken with a deep sleep and dismissed her alarm clock. In no time at all, her heavy eyelids shut and she was completely out of consciousness.

A pounding on her door startled Jordyn awake.

"Jordyn, it's time to go." Kathleen spoke abruptly. Jordyn struggled to turn onto her back and slowly forced her eyes open to try and assess the situation.

"Are you ready?" Kathleen's voice rose in frustration. Jordyn placed a hand against each side of the brim of her nose to rub her eyes and then continued outward across her whole face. There was no chance that she could function like this. Plus, she would rather not deal with all the feelings that came up at church. It was risky, but Jordyn figured her mom couldn't get much angrier.

"I don't feel well." Jordyn groaned.

This was the complete truth to Jordyn and she felt like she sounded very convincing.

Either Kathleen was too upset to care, or she didn't believe her.

"So you're not going to come?"

Jordyn didn't know how to stop the wedge that was forming between them. A simple "no" was all she could get out.

"We will see you in a few hours, then." The disappointment in her mom's voice was resounding.

Jordyn hated creating distance between them, but she would have to deal with that later. Right now, the only thing she had the energy for was to melt back into her sheets and pull her blankets up to her neck.

For the rest of Sunday, Jordyn lay low in her room. Occasionally, she came out to go to the bathroom or to grab a snack from the pantry, but other than that, she remained hidden away downstairs. In the evening, she spent some time sitting in Blake's room. All she had the strength to do was sit there with her eyes closed, breathing in and out. Blake had been gone for too long now, and she found herself grasping at anything that would remind her of him. Jordyn reached across the bed for Blake's pillow. She held it very carefully, as if it was fragile, and carried it into her room.

Very softly, she lowered his pillow over hers and laid down on her side. She took in a deep breath of his scent as she pulled up her covers. At some point his smell would fade away, but for now, it was as close as she could get to him. She never understood how Blake could have chosen to leave her, but she was understanding more of how awful it must have felt for him to feel like he was completely alone. She was feeling more like that every day; the continual anguish and misery that made it seem like happiness was truly a thing of the past. In desperation to avoid the pain, Jordyn shut her eyes and dozed off for the night.

Jordyn's eyelids fluttered and she turned toward her alarm clock. She squinted her eyes in an attempt to fix the blurry red numbers to see what time it was. Eventually, her eyes cooperated and showed 10:03. More detective work was needed to see if that was a.m. or p.m. She rolled over and saw light around her dark grey curtains and concluded that it was morning time. This was confirmed further when she heard a loud thump. As she listened closely to figure out what the noise was, she heard another clunk and the sound of her parents talking. The noises seemed close, but she couldn't quite figure it out by listening alone. She decided she would peek out of her room to see what was happening.

As she opened her bedroom door, she realized the sounds were closer than she thought. Jordyn looked to the left and saw her dad's legs coming out of Blake's room. Jordyn's expression became puzzled trying to decipher the situation. As she heard more thuds and bumps coming from Blake's room, she felt an urgent need to know what was going on.

"What are you doing?" Jordyn's tone came out in an accusing manner.

"Good morning, Jordyn." Fred peeked out from around Blake's doorway. He smiled before he continued speaking, although Jordyn could see that he had been crying.

"We decided that it was time to go through Blake's room."

Jordyn's whole body became tense and she couldn't decide whether she needed to scream or throw up. She walked into Blake's doorway in order to see what he meant, exactly. Anxiety crept through her as she saw boxes lining the perimeter of his room. Jordyn couldn't fathom what her parents could possibly be doing. Blake's room was more than just his stuff. Blake's room was her sanctuary. It was her place to be as close to him as possible. It was a place she could go to remember him and imagine him still with her. Often she had laid on his bed and talked as if he was there listening to her. Now his blankets and sheets were in a pile on the ground, and there was just a bare mattress against the wall.

Her emotions built up from zero to one hundred in a matter of seconds. All that came out of her was a betrayed whisper.

"How could you?"

Jordyn turned and ran straight into her room. She pushed the door closed as hard as she possibly could. In her anger, she hit the wall next to her with her fists and her push-pin board came crashing to the ground. Jordyn dove onto her knees and scooped up her picture of Blake and the note he left for her and held them tightly against her chest.

Fred slowly cracked open her bedroom door.

"Jordyn, sweetie. I'm sorry if we did something wrong." He was always such a gentle giant. Jordyn knew that her response was too harsh for what he deserved, but it didn't change the fact that it still came out of her mouth.

"Just go away!"

The sting in her soul was too powerful for her rational mind to be in control right now. As Fred closed the door, Jordyn felt even worse now because of the way she had just treated her father. Why couldn't she do anything right anymore? Blake's suicide took away more than just Blake from her. It took away everything that was good inside of her. She was so broken that there didn't seem to be any way to sort through the millions of pieces and then there was still the huge undertaking of putting any of them back together. Jordyn didn't know how she could get any lower than in that moment on her bedroom floor, but she was now no longer too naive to realize that it was a possibility.

Chapter 13

Christmas is supposed to be a time of joy, kindness, holly jolly laughs, and homemade cookies around a fire. There was zero of that to be found in the Alden household. Sure, Jordyn's parents tried their best to be merry and bright around her, but when there is such a tragic elephant in the room, nothing can be done to lighten the mood.

Nate and Dillon both came over for Christmas Eve dinner. It was the first time Jordyn had seen either of them for a month. They stayed right on queue of the day with very surface-like conversations—nothing too deep, or else it would ruin Christmas. It didn't matter to Jordyn what anyone did or did not say or what they did or did not do, because every day was ruined from now until the end of time. Memories from the past year haunted her at every turn.

Jordyn sat on their living room couch and looked up at the fake Christmas tree. A flashback played through her mind of Blake nearly tipping the whole tree over onto their dog, Midnight, by running into the already broken tree-stand. The gingerbread ornament Brady had made in elementary school had fallen right by Midnight's head, causing her to jump up and run away into the kitchen immediately. It was a moment where they both had uncontrollably burst out laughing.

Jordyn contemplated how many good times they had together in that past year before his suicide. She wondered if he had realized that there were so many happy moments that they had shared together. Maybe he couldn't recognize that anything was actually good with his depression overshadowing him. If only he could have seen that there was good— maybe then he would still be there with her.

Blake had always been able to tell when she was unhappy and would always get it out of her somehow—whether it was bribing her with chocolate, tickling her until she cracked, or just the simple look he gave her. He would have been the perfect sounding board for Jordyn right now. She was feeling even more down today because Livie had just sent her a text with full bragging rights. Steve had asked Ashley out on a date that they went on together yesterday, so Jordyn lost the bet. It wasn't the fact that she lost—five dollars and her pride wasn't the issue at all. Jordyn was sad because they had made it on a date before she and Greg went on their date, which really should have been no surprise at all since no plans ever were made. Still, she had hoped that he would call her over the break and sweep her off her feet. Jordyn fell asleep Christmas Eve defeated—knowing that she was definitely not living in a fairytale.

To top the rest of the holiday off, it was really strange for Jordyn to open presents Christmas morning without Blake there. Nothing felt right. Every year, Kathleen would take a photo of all the kids with their presents gathered around the tree. This year was just another awful reminder of how alone Jordyn felt when her mom pulled out her camera to take the annual photo. Jordyn sat on the big empty couch and attempted a smile. She wasn't sure how it turned out, but she was sure that it wasn't going to look very convincing. Jordyn touched her new sweatshirt as she remembered that morning's sadness, and tucked it away. Presents used to be exciting, but she didn't want anything for Christmas other than Blake being there with her.

The one good thing about this week was there was no therapy due to the holiday. She would definitely count that as a blessing. When her parents were distracted with a neighbor visiting them, Jordyn snuck away to be by herself downstairs. She swept past Blake's door and with one look at a box poking out, her blood ran cold and her heart felt chilled. As she turned away to enter her room, her eyes focused on the unopened letter on her desk from Brady that was brutally taunting her. She felt ashamed to open it up, because she had broken her promises to him. Not only had she not written him a letter yet, but the words that they had repeated together at the airport could not be further from the truth. She couldn't do this.

Slowly Jordyn made her way to her desk and lowered herself onto the chair. She picked up the letter and read her name on the front of the envelope over and over again. Would there be encouragement written in there? Would he sound mad that he hadn't heard from her? Would he be open to her about how he was doing, or would he try to keep things near the surface just like the rest of her family was doing?

Jordyn took a deep breath in, and as she exhaled, she ripped the top of the envelope open. The thumping in her chest became more intense every second, but she pulled the letter out anyway. Her eyes automatically filled up with tears when she saw *Dear Jordyn,* and then the rest of the words blurred away. Emotions rushed through her like an ocean wave crashing against the sand. With every tear released, the wave crashed down with more force. How could two words overtake her this way? The words began to come into focus now.

Hey, favorite sister!

I haven't heard from you and I wish I was there with you.

She rapidly folded the letter down and put it down on her desk because her soul couldn't take anymore. Every inch of her was so exhausted from constantly feeling—physically, emotionally, and mentally. She just needed to stop feeling. Jordyn curled up into a ball on her bed with Blake's pillow in her arms and drifted off to sleep, tears flowing.

She woke up to a ding coming from her phone. Jordyn reached out to her bedside table and rummaged around until she felt the square, smooth surface. One notification showed: a text message from Benson.

Thought anymore about my party tomorrow night?

It wasn't even about how she thought her parents would react to her going to a party, but she didn't think she was even capable of being around a lot of people. Her answer was simple and easy.

I don't think I can come.

Not even thirty seconds passed before he responded.

Here's my address for when you change your mind.

Jordyn couldn't help but grin as her phone beeped again with a text message with his address. It seemed like he didn't give up easily. Still, she felt pretty confident in her decision not to even try to go to the party. Jordyn grew more tired every day trying to keep up appearances.

* * *

The next day came and started out as typically as any of the past weekdays had. Jordyn slept in as late as she wanted to, and then she continued to lounge about in her sweatpants for the remainder of the day. It was nice to have an uneventful day. As Jordyn started up the stairs to go make a sandwich for a late lunch, something caught her eye outside the window. She turned to see her dad packing boxes into his car. Jordyn knew it was boxes full of Blake's stuff.

"There you are." Kathleen spoke. "Do you need anything? Dad and I are just leaving to run some errands. We are also going to dinner with grandma and grandpa, so we won't be home until around eight tonight."

Jordyn wished her mom just would tell her the whole truth and admit that they were leaving to get rid of all of Blake's things. She couldn't believe that they would want to leave him as just a memory so soon. She definitely wasn't ready to move on.

"I'm fine."

Jordyn spoke without looking Kathleen in the eyes. She made her way to the fridge and pulled out the cheese and lunch meat. Jordyn continued to be busy so it didn't seem awkward for her to not meet her mother's glances.

"Okay. We will see you later tonight, then."

Her mom's voice sounded sullen. Jordyn kept her eyes on her sandwich. As soon as the crisp sound of the front door closing signaled that she was alone, she tasted salty tears on her lips as she opened her mouth to take a bite out of her sandwich.

What more would she be forced to endure? The emptiness inside her grew and grew. Jordyn sat there at the kitchen table, completely helpless. The room almost spun as she thought about how out of control her life was. Would she ever be able to get out of all these external forces swirling around her? But wait—what if there was something that she could control? Jordyn reached into her back pocket and pulled out her cell phone. She took charge and pressed buttons with great determination.

I don't know how you knew I would, but I've changed my mind. I don't have a ride though. Would you be willing to pick me up?

She needed Benson to respond to her. She wanted so badly to control something in her life, but his house was too far to walk. She tried to talk her impatience away because his party didn't start for another hour. Of course he would see it in time and respond. She threw the rest of her sandwich in the garbage and proceeded downstairs to begin the process of looking presentable.

Jordyn thumbed through her closet and decided on a warm blue sweater and jeans. She wasn't feeling too energetic and lively, so mascara and lip gloss were the perfect amount of makeup without going overboard. Jordyn finished up by brushing through her hair and pulling half of it up. There. She picked her phone up off the desk, hoping to see the sweet sight of a notification, but to her dismay, there weren't any. Why was this the time that Benson wasn't responding right away?

Out of frustration, Jordyn slammed her phone down onto the desk. Her arm swept across the wooden surface, and Blake's watch crashed against the wall and onto the floor under the desk. Jordyn paused and covered her mouth with her hands. Why was she a tornado, negatively affecting everything around her? She wished that she could separate the fierce winds of this tragedy from her to only exist and swirl around her, but she had become a part of them. How much ruin and destruction would she leave behind?

Jordyn pushed her chair to the side and knelt down in front of the desk to reach Blake's watch. She examined the face and kept turning it to make sure every inch was okay. A loud knock of the front door startled her, so she set the watch down and hurried up the stairs. She peeked out the peephole to see Benson standing outside. She ran quickly down to her room to grab her purse and phone before answering the door. Out of breath and with nerves catching up to her, she turned the doorknob. Benson held his arm out to escort her.

"Your chariot awaits."

Chapter 14

Benson led the way, and as Jordyn entered through his front door, she felt a tinge of regret. She wasn't really sure what she would be walking into at this party, and she knew her parents definitely wouldn't be pleased when they came home to find her gone. Thankfully, Benson had picked her up before other people arrived, so she reasoned that it would be easy for her to relax and enjoy herself without becoming overwhelmed by a huge crowd of people.

Jordyn looked around the kitchen and immediately began to admire the beauty and how spacious it was. The kitchen opened up into the dining room and the family room which made it perfect for a party. It was all easily three times the size of corresponding spaces in her own house. Benson threw his keys onto the kitchen counter and bent down to reach into the bottom cabinet.

"I'm just needing to spread out all of the food on the island. Would you mind grabbing the desserts out of the fridge?"

Jordyn was grateful to have something to do with her hands to distract her.

"Sure thing!" Jordyn replied, trying to sound helpful.

"Thanks! I'll be right back. I left the rest in the truck." Benson disappeared through the entryway.

Jordyn opened the fridge, and grabbed the large container at the front that she guessed was the desserts. She smelled cheesecake squares as she took the lid off the container. She wasn't hungry since she had eaten not too long ago, but she was sure by the end of the night some of these would find their way into her stomach. Her thoughts wandered to Blake, as they normally did, and she wondered if he ever stood exactly where she was standing now. She liked being somewhere new that tied her a little closer to him.

Benson came stumbling in through the front door with his hands full. Jordyn hurried toward him to help.

"Here, let me carry something for you!"

He kicked backward to close the door as he chuckled. Jordyn grabbed the pizza boxes on top of his pile.

"I hate to go out into the cold to get them, so I was trying to do it all in one trip. Thanks, Jordyn."

There was his smile again that caused Jordyn's heart to race every single time. She looked away a little too soon, though, and walked over to the counter and set the pizzas down.

"Hey, I want to show you something."

Benson motioned over to the hallway as he started walking.

"I have some pictures of Blake that I was looking through and thought you might be interested in seeing."

Jordyn smiled at the thought and followed him through the hallway to what she could only assume was his bedroom. He had an opened shoebox on his bed with pictures scattered around. She stood in the doorway looking around at all of the baseball memorabilia plastered to his walls. Blake loved the Yankees, too, and Jordyn was certain he spent quite a few afternoons admiring Benson's collection.

"Here, come take a look!"

Benson was already sitting on the edge of his bed and patted the spot next to him, expectantly. There was only a small space for her to sit if she wanted to see the pictures, so Jordyn sat with her leg touching Benson's. He handed her a pile of four-by-six photos of him and Blake together over the course of their friendship. It was nice to see new pictures of Blake. Pretty much every picture she had of him was already committed to memory with how many times she had thumbed through them.

It was still hard for Jordyn to believe that Blake was really gone and that she wouldn't see him in person again. Pictures were literally the only way she *could* see him now. Not that she wanted to die anytime soon, but she was jealous that so many other people would probably die before her and get to see him again before she would. Jordyn didn't know exactly how it all worked, but she did feel deep within her that they would be reunited in Heaven someday. Despite her recent lack of faith, she knew this life couldn't be all there was. It didn't make sense to Jordyn that you could love someone so much just to have them disappear forever. Blake had to live past these photos.

Benson's hand grazed hers when they were switching photos to look at. Benson turned toward Jordyn and the look in his eyes made Jordyn's heart pound hard and fast.

"I've really enjoyed spending time with you, Jordyn."

Since she had never been kissed, she wasn't sure how she knew he was getting ready to kiss her, but she knew.

"Me too."

Her answer was short and she averted his gaze and glued her eyes back down to the photos in her hands and tried to act as casual as she could under the circumstances. Benson began testing the boundaries by putting his arm around Jordyn's shoulders. She was starting to feel uneasy being alone with him, especially sitting on his bed together. As Jordyn was running ideas through her head on how to save face and get herself out of this situation, she heard the front door slam shut.

"Yo, Benson! We're here and we've got the goods!"

Jordyn didn't recognize the voice, but she loved whoever it was for helping her get out of being alone with Benson. It wasn't that she was revolted at the thought of kissing him, but she didn't feel particularly comfortable being completely alone with him like this, much less on his bed—and she wasn't even sure if she wanted to kiss him. Benson gave Jordyn a disappointed look and they both got up from the bed. Jordyn felt increasingly awkward at how it probably looked as she followed Benson out of his room and through the hallway.

"Oh, you have a girl over! We're sorry to have interrupted whatever you two were doing back there!"

Jordyn didn't know the two boys standing there, but her face immediately flushed bright red with their comment and assumption.

"Shut up. Jordyn, this is Dallin and Fiz. Boys, this is Blake's sister."

Dallin and Fiz both softened in their stance. Jordyn attempted to continue to act cool and collected as if she was capable of handling this awkward situation.

"It's nice to meet you both. Fiz is an interesting name?"

"We call him that because he has all the connections to our drinks."

For the whole minute she'd been in the kitchen, Jordyn had been too distracted and embarrassed to notice the stack of beer cases on the counter until now. Panic immediately set in. If she knew that there would be drinking at this party, she wouldn't have come. Benson noticed Jordyn take an abrupt step back.

Jordyn felt her body tighten.

"Don't worry," Benson spoke reassuringly, "you don't have to drink. We couldn't ever get your brother to drink with us, either."

Benson and his friends laughed and Jordyn felt somewhat relieved by the fact that Blake hadn't been secretly drinking. That would have added a whole new layer onto his suicide that she just couldn't handle at the moment. She reasoned that if Blake could hang out with them at parties without drinking, so could she.

The doorbell rang, and as Benson went to let in a group of friends, Jordyn went and sat on the couch to observe. She didn't always come off as a shy and reserved person, but her comfort was in keeping to herself until she was comfortable. Jordyn quietly watched as each group came through the front door. She recognized one or two people every few minutes and occasionally someone would come say hi to her. Maybe this party wouldn't be so bad.

Things started out fairly tame, but people quickly busted the beer cases open and began drinking like they were parched. It had been an hour since Dallin and Fiz got there, and Benson hadn't been over to talk to her since. This party was not turning out as she had imagined, although she had to admit that she hadn't really thought about what it would be like—she had just decided to come on a whim. Jordyn stood up and walked without drawing attention to herself as she made her way to the back deck for some fresh air. She leaned against the railing and took a deep breath in. A crashing sound on the sliding door behind Jordyn disturbed her peaceful moment. Jordyn turned to see that it was Benson, Dallin, and Fiz making faces at her against the glass. She could tell that the alcohol was in full effect and that they were being crazier than they normally would. Benson slid open the door on his third attempt and stumbled out to talk to her.

"Hey, girrl." He slurred.

Jordyn nodded her head to him in acknowledgement. She wondered how drunk he was.

"You know what? You should totally have some of this." Benson offered a half-empty can to her in what he must've thought was an enticing way.

"No, thanks."

Jordyn spoke as politely as she could muster.

"Whatever. Here!"

Benson swung his beer can slopilly toward her, accidentally splashing some onto her sweater.

"Oh, oops. Just lick it off . . . " he guffawed.

Benson continued laughing as Jordyn held her sweater out with one hand and tried wiping the beer off with her other hand.

"You're such a chicken. Bawk bawk bawk." Benson flapped his elbows around trying to imitate a chicken to emphasize his point.

Jordyn stood still and silent as anger began to rise within her. Benson leaned up against the railing next to her and his demeanor changed.

"It's good not to feel for a while. That's what you gotta do to survive the crap in this world."

It was a tempting thought, but Jordyn knew that drinking was a line she didn't want to cross. There was no way she ever wanted to act the way he was treating her right now.

"I'm fine."

Jordyn looked straight at Benson, noticing his eyes were

glazed.

"You're no fun, Blake." Benson drawled.

Jordyn gasped at Benson's mistake. It took her completely off guard. He hadn't noticed her reaction because he had closed his eyes in a stupor, letting Jordyn quickly and quietly walk away from him into the house. She scooped her purse off the fireplace mantle and found a bathroom through the hallway next to Benson's bedroom for another bathroom breakdown. Why did she think that coming here would help her feel better? It turned out that this party didn't help the emptiness go away at all. She wondered if Blake had felt out of place at these parties too. She was also ashamed of the feelings she had started having toward Benson, since they were obviously a huge mistake on her part as well.

Desperately, Jordyn reached inside her purse and pulled out her phone. She had hit a breaking point and with tears rolling down her face, she sought the courage to take control again with a text.

I need saving.

Chapter 15

Jordyn sat on Benson's front porch in near darkness as the sun was fading behind the mountain. She couldn't help but take in the beauty of it. Even more beautiful than the sun setting was the sight of the white Honda Civic as it pulled up to the curb. Before Jordyn could even get up to hop in the car, Greg parked and rushed over to her on the porch.

When Jordyn saw him coming toward her, the tears that were still near the surface came pouring down just as quickly as he had come to rescue her. Greg pulled Jordyn in close to his chest and held her tightly. Feeling completely safe in his arms only caused her tears to flow more freely. With everything so wrong around her and inside of her, it was strangely perfect to be in his arms right now. Greg looked down at Jordyn and rested his head on top of hers.

He pulled away slightly and lifted Jordyn's chin up to have her face him. With his strong hands, Greg gently wiped away the streams on her cheeks. Greg's pureness always made an impression on Jordyn.

"Let's get you out of here."

Jordyn only hoped he could see the gratitude in her eyes.

Greg opened the passenger door for Jordyn. After getting in, he reached over and grabbed Jordyn's hand. She swallowed and squeezed his hand.

"I really don't deserve you being my hero all of the time."

Greg squeezed her hand back.

"Don't ever say that, Jordyn. You deserve the very best. I want to always be here for you . . . if you'll let me."

Jordyn knew that he was being honest. She decided to take a leap of faith with him.

"I'm just so broken. Everything is falling apart and I can't seem to stop it. Nothing is right anymore. Nothing."

She must have been extra hydrated today because the tears just kept coming.

"You are going through one of the most terrible things I have ever heard of. I don't know how you could be anything but broken. I know I don't understand, and I know that I wasn't close to Blake, but I do know I care a whole lot about you. I'm here for you, Jordyn."

Jordyn could tell that Greg was referring to her spending time with Benson. She wiped her face with her sleeve and cleared her throat.

"Coming to this party was a huge mistake. I was so angry that my parents cleaned out Blake's room because his room was a special escape for me. And then Ashley and Steve went on a date and I hadn't heard from you at all during the break. I was losing it and I had to do something. I don't even feel like I can think clearly lately."

The edges of Greg's mouth dipped down.

"I'm so sorry, Jordyn. First, I'm sorry that your parents did that. I know they love you, so they must not have known how much it meant to you."

Jordyn valued Greg's insights and his authentic attitude helped her feel grounded.

"I know they do. They're just on this whole other level than me and it's been hard."

Greg squeezed her hand again and continued.

"Second, I feel awful that we didn't talk this week. My parents surprised our family with a cabin trip for the holiday and we just got back today. I guess they wanted us to be off our phones and to spend time with them for once instead of being distracted by our friends."

Greg's warm smile returned as he looked at her. Jordyn knew that she was one of his distractions and her body's usual reaction of blushing came once again.

"I've actually been thinking a lot about our date and I can't wait to take you. I would take you right now, but I've been planning something special for you."

Jordyn felt a little foolish. It was unfair for her to get discouraged without knowing all of the facts. It was too easy for her to be self-absorbed right now and she knew she wasn't thinking straight all the time. It was time for her to put Greg's feelings higher on her priority list.

She spoke with conviction now. "This is going to sound really off, but will you do me a favor?"

Greg looked intently in her eyes, waiting to hear what he could do for her.

"Could we postpone our date for a few more months?"

Greg said no words, but his confused look spoke clearly enough.

"I just don't feel like it's fair to you while I'm like this. If you really are making things special for me, which I have no doubt that you are, I need to be in a better headspace about things. I have some work to do on and for myself."

Greg turned the keys in the ignition. His tone hardened.

"Don't shut me out, Jordyn."

Jordyn reached over and turned the keys backward before Greg could put the car into drive.

"No, no, no. You aren't understanding what I mean. This isn't me shutting you out. I haven't even gotten out of bed for the past week until now, Greg. You know it's bad if I just came to a random party to try and feel better. When you just said that I deserve the best, I know you meant it. But Greg, *you* also deserve the best and I am not ready to be that yet even for myself. I've been so stuck, and I'm not sure how long it takes, but I want to try to take some steps forward."

Greg softened with understanding and he again took Jordyn's hand.

"I will wait as long as I need to, but I'm not going anywhere. You don't have to do this alone. Example number one—I will walk you to Sunday School tomorrow and we can sit together."

Jordyn was hesitant.

"I'm not sure about that one. Church is really hard for me and I haven't been for a few weeks."

"It's okay. You're not alone, remember? You said you wanted to take some steps, and this one seems like it could help."

Jordyn couldn't deny Greg's sincerity.

"Okay. I will try." she agreed.

Chapter 16

There were nerves running through Jordyn's whole body as she entered through the glass doors of the church building with her parents. It was unlike her family to be late to the service, but she could hear singing, which meant the meeting had just started. As they sat in the back row of the chapel, Jordyn took a deep breath and her arms and shoulders began to relax. It was better to sit back here where she could focus more on herself than everyone else, who she thought would be judging her.

As announcements were being made over the pulpit, Jordyn closed her eyes. This time it wasn't because she was trying to escape, but she wanted to try and remember how church felt before Blake was gone. Even though it had only been a few months, it seemed like a lifetime ago. She thought about how she used to be uplifted while singing the hymns, how she had enjoyed doodling little notes during the speakers, and how she had felt the spirit and genuinely felt good at church. How could one tragic decision from her brother change so much?

Jordyn opened her eyes and observed some of the families around where they were sitting as the service continued. First, there was the Hitchcock family sitting in the row in front of them. They had a little boy and girl who were driving

Hot Wheels cars up and down the bench. Their mom would occasionally lean over and shush them, but the kids didn't seem to care as they kept playing imaginatively together. Jordyn didn't know them well, but when she handed the little boy a car that dropped down near her, she felt a pure love for him as he shyly accepted it back.

The Baileys sat on the row diagonal from Jordyn. It was Jenny Bailey and her husband who were in their mid-thirties. Jordyn knew Jenny since she was in charge of her girl's youth group at church. Jordyn noticed her delightful smile and beaming face as she continued to watch them. She couldn't quite take her eyes off of Jenny. Jordyn remembered back to when Jenny had opened up to the girls about how she hadn't been able to have children, but she had always testified of her faith in God's plan for her. Jordyn wasn't sure what that must be like, but she was sure that even through Jenny's pain, she was finding the good at church. She could see it.

The organist sat down on the bench and began to play. Jordyn decided she was going to try singing again like she used to. If she really was going to take steps forward, participating seemed like a good place to start. She opened the hymnal and flipped through its pages until she found number 220.

Savior, may I learn to love thee,
Walk the path that thou hast shown,

The first two lines of the song nearly left Jordyn breathless and took her completely off guard. It pierced a place inside of her heart that had been hidden ever since she found out about Blake's suicide. All of the despair and problems it brought had overshadowed how much she desperately needed a Savior. Jordyn couldn't carry this burden on her shoulders for another second.

Pause to help and lift another,
Finding strength beyond my own.

Jordyn was slipping more and more every single day and the only way out would be to find some strength beyond her own. Tingles went up her arms and into her chest.

Savior, may I learn to love thee—
Lord, I would follow thee.

She realized she had a choice to make. Either Jordyn could continue on the path she was on right now, which she could only imagine led to dark abyss and more emptiness, if that was even possible—or—she had to deliberately choose to follow the Lord.

Who am I to judge another
When I walk imperfectly?

Never had words been more true. It felt like every step she made had been imperfect these past few months.

In the quiet heart is hidden
Sorrow that the eye can't see.

This hymn spoke specifically to her. There was sorrow that filled every crevice of her aching heart.

Who am I to judge another?
Lord, I would follow thee.

Jordyn knew she needed to start dealing with Blake's death. She needed The Lord, indeed.

I would be my brother's keeper;
I would learn the healer's art.

Blake. She would have been Blake's keeper if she had known. But she had no idea. It hadn't been her fault at all. She loved her brother, and he had known that.

There was a rush of love that swept over her whole body. Comfort. Release. Rest. Succor. Tears. Jordyn was unable to continue singing.

To the wounded and the weary
I would show a gentle heart.

Blake was wounded, and it left her more wounded than she could have ever imagined a person being. Jordyn wished she would have known he was wounded. She would have shown him a gentle heart. Maybe she could show them both a gentle heart now by actually working through this.

I would be my brother's keeper—
Lord, I would follow thee.

How could she be Blake's keeper even now? She hoped following The Savior would be enough.

Savior, may I love my brother
As I know thou lovest me,

Jordyn followed along as her emotions kept her from singing. She felt fully encompassed by Heavenly Father's love, and, with the warmth inside of her, she wouldn't be surprised if Blake was right there with her.

Find in thee my strength, my beacon,
For thy servant I would be.

The way Jordyn was going to find the strength she needed was in her Savior. This key fact was what she was missing this whole time. She wasn't alone.

Savior, may I love my brother—
Lord, I would follow thee.

Lord, I will follow thee. Jordyn silently resolved in her heart that she would. An overwhelming blanket of peace engulfed her. Peace. This was a new feeling to Jordyn, but she fully recognized it with the Spirit's help.

Left in awe and amazement, Jordyn sat quietly on the bench

as the prayer was offered and then continued to be still as the congregation was filing out of the chapel. Greg cleared his throat to get Jordyn's attention. He offered his hand to walk her to Sunday School, as promised.

"Are you okay?" He asked tentatively.

Jordyn thought about his question seriously, and felt gratitude as she thought about how to answer. She probably wouldn't have come today if he hadn't urged her to take the step. She looked up at him, hoping to convey the ray of hope she felt.

"For the first time in a long time, I think I will be."

Chapter 17

Jordyn rolled over and stretched high above her head. She lingered in the warmth of the blankets for a few extra moments before tossing them off of her legs. After her sacred experience yesterday, Jordyn knew that living her life wouldn't automatically be easy, but she could see a small beam of light through all the cloudy gray. She wasn't going to let the end of Blake's life be the end of hers—because although she was still alive, she hadn't been truly living.

Slowly, Jordyn lowered her knees onto the floor and whispered a simple and honest prayer.

"Heavenly Father, please help me today. And every day. Amen."

Even though that was all she could utter at the moment, she knew it was enough and immediately felt a wave a peace flow through her heart just like she had felt yesterday during the hymn. Jordyn placed her hand on her heart and stroked her chest. She could get used to experiencing this. It was the only feeling that hadn't completely taken her energy away. Jordyn stood up, and with the same hand that had been on her heart, she stroked Blake's pillow.

"I love you."

What followed was strange but welcomed. Instead of feeling

an overwhelming aching sadness, Jordyn felt a joyful love for Blake as she spoke those three words. She was obviously sad, but it was amazing to her that at that moment, she could think about him with a positive love being the main force in her heart. There was a new space created that seemed capable of holding both sadness and love, and she was beginning to realize that it was okay to feel them both.

Jordyn unzipped the front pocket of her backpack and again placed Blake's watch inside. She wanted a part of him with her as she was returning to school after the break. It was time for her to stare all of the missing assignments and tests in the face that had been looming over her for the past few months. Jordyn had no desire before now to deal with anything that Blake's death had brought into her life, but she knew it was time. She had been lost for too long, and the only way to be found was to stop avoiding everything and allowing misery to completely overshadow her. If she was being truthful to herself, she hadn't wanted to deal with anything and hadn't even wanted to begin to heal before yesterday. Jordyn had thought that healing was equal to forgetting or moving on, but she was starting to realize that healing and sadness could coexist. The fear of that was starting to dissipate and Jordyn thought that God really was capable of helping her, even through this.

Kathleen dropped Jordyn off at school in the same spot she did every day.

"I hope you have a good day today." She uttered the typical farewell.

Jordyn knew that their relationship had been strained lately, but she was determined to put forth more effort.

"Thanks, mom. I'm going to try. I hope you have a good day, too."

She watched as the corner of her mom's lips lifted up into a smile with her sincere response. Jordyn already felt and was grateful for the help from her prayer that morning.

Jordyn hopped out of the car, but instead of going inside the high school building, she headed straight to the Seminary building. Hopefully she would be able to catch Brother Harley before class started. When she saw his office door open, Jordyn subconsciously walked quicker in anticipation.

Jordyn knocked gently on the door to announce herself. Brother Harley took a look over his shoulder and smiled wide when he saw her in the doorway.

"Good morning, Jordyn! It's so nice to see you this morning. Let me just finish writing the thought down for today's class."

His positive outlook and friendliness made him easily the favorite teacher with most of the students. Jordyn remained silent while he vigorously wrote on a half sheet of paper. Once he turned back toward her, she spoke up.

"I'm really sorry that I haven't been coming to class. The truth is that I haven't even taken a look at the scriptures you suggested for me. I really haven't been doing much of anything—but I am here now."

Compassion filled Brother Harley's countenance.

"You have zero reason to say sorry to me, Jordyn. I'm so glad that you're here because I think you'll enjoy the lesson today as it will relate to what you're going through—*but* you have no reason to feel bad or guilty for struggling through things lately." He paused before continuing kindly, "Did you know that there are numerous people in the scriptures who struggled with their faith at times and had really difficult trials? Often it helped them grow stronger and learn important things to become who God knew they could be. I truly believe that God has amazing things in store for you too, Jordyn."

Jordyn had never thought of learning and becoming better from losing Blake. She also hadn't realized the burden that her guilt had become—subtly suffocating her and nearly squeezing her completely away from God and the thought of making it through this trial. Maybe broken wasn't intended to be a permanent state.

"Now, how about you help me place these papers on all of the desks before the rest of the students make their way in?"

Jordyn nodded and grabbed the stack of papers from Brother Harley before heading into the classroom. A few students trickled in as she walked down each row and placed a paper on each desk. When she was done, she sat down in her seat and pulled her scriptures out of her backpack. She opened up the front cover and removed the list of scriptures that Brother Harley had given her months ago and turned to the first scripture on the list.

Matthew 11:28-30

28. Come unto me, all ye that labour and are heavy laden, and I will give you rest.

29. Take my yoke upon you, and learn of me; for I am meek and lowly in heart: and ye shall find rest unto your souls.

30. For my yoke is easy, and my burden is light.

Certain words jumped off of the page as she read each verse. The same words kept standing out, and each one entered the depths of her soul:

Come, labour, heavy, **rest**.

Take, learn, meek, lowly, **rest**.

Easy. Light.

If coming unto Christ meant that the heaviness of her life and the harsh labor that was grief could be transformed into easy, light, rest through Him, Jordyn knew that all she could do now was trust in the Lord.

Jordyn's thoughts were interrupted by the bell and Brother Harley asking the class to turn to Matthew fourteen in their scriptures. She turned the three pages from where she had been to chapter fourteen.

"Before reading the verses of the story we are going to focus on, I just want to give you a little background to set this up fully. This was the day that Jesus took and broke the five loaves of bread and two fishes. We learn in verse twenty-one that it fed five thousand men plus women and children. Would you say that this was a miracle?"

There was an audible "yes" throughout the class in response to Brother Harley's question.

"Now, imagine seeing that miracle happen. Close your eyes and picture how in the beginning, you would have been questioning how Jesus would be able to feed all the people you see. Then picture the amazement of being one of his disciples passing around the baskets of broken food and witnessing firsthand that there was plenty to go around and to spare."

Brother Harley paused for a moment as they imagined the scenario.

"What do you think this would do for your testimony?"

Jordyn opened her eyes and saw her classmate, Brian, near the front of the class raised his hand to answer.

"I would think it would grow since you saw it with your own eyes."

"I imagine that as well. Okay, so now to our story for the day. The disciples had just been with Jesus witnessing this amazing miracle, and then he had them get on a ship while he went into the mountains to pray. After a while, Jesus walked on the sea toward their ship. At first, they didn't know it was him and they were afraid. But Jesus announces himself in verse twenty-seven and says, 'Be of good cheer; it is I; be not afraid.' Peter, one of his disciples then asks if he could come on the water with Jesus and walk with him. That takes faith, right? I mean, I've never walked on water, but I would assume you would have to be on a spiritual high from experiencing the loaves-of-bread-and-fish-miracle to have that kind of faith. Jesus tells him to come, and Peter starts walking on the water toward Jesus. Amazing, right?"

Jordyn was intrigued and caught up in imagining being with Jesus during these stories. She was picturing being right there watching it all and nodded that it would be truly amazing.

"But. This is the way verse thirty begins: But. "But when he saw the wind boisterous, he was afraid; and beginning to sink, he cried, saying, Lord, save me." The wind started and Peter became afraid and started to sink. This is huge, everyone! If you can't quite imagine walking on water with a storm starting to brew, what kinds of winds do we experience in our lives that could cause us to sink?"

Brother Harley looked toward Jordyn with that same compassionate look that he gave her earlier in the office. She knew that he meant Blake's suicide. Students raised their hands and Brother Harley made a list on the whiteboard of all the winds of life that they were mentioning. Jordyn closed her eyes and pictured being out on the water and seeing her life swirling around her like boisterous winds. She saw Blake disappearing around her. She saw herself crying desperately and alone in her room. She saw her parents and Brady and everyone who

110

was crammed in the church at Blake's funeral.

"How easy would it be to sink while these winds are surrounding you? What about literally hours after witnessing a miracle? Peter *still* started sinking! We are going to sink, class. It's going to happen. Don't think that you are going to be the one person who is free from wind shaking your faith, because it can happen and will happen."

The class was silent and sullen, but Jordyn knew that Brother Harley was about to turn things around.

"Don't you dare fear, though. Just like Jesus announced to his disciples in the ship, "Be of good cheer; it is I; be not afraid." I am here to tell you that it is okay to start sinking and there is a way to walk on the water again. Do you remember Peter's last words? He cried out saying, "Lord, save me." Peter focused back on the Savior. This is the key, guys! We will sink, but we need to keep our focus on the Savior just like Peter did. The next verse says that *immediately,* Jesus stretched forth his hand and caught him. Immediately. I have learned this truth in my own life and I know that Christ is right there stretching forth his hand in the storms of our lives."

Again, Brother Harley made his last remark while glancing at Jordyn. As he continued speaking, his voice and the whole classroom around her faded into the background. It was just her sinking in the deep water with Jesus reaching his hand forward to catch her. She could literally feel the Savior lifting her out of the water. It was going to be nice to finally dry off and have refuge from the storms of Blake's suicide in and through Christ.

A Note to Readers

Life is full of choices. Choices define which direction we go. My experience losing Blake is just that—my own personal experience. I know not everyone will go through the same trials, or even the same healing process. But my purpose in writing this book was to give hope and validation to those of us who are experiencing and have experienced the harsh storms that life brings—which should include just about everyone. Even after I made the choice to move forward—without forgetting Blake—it was still hard. There were still rough days. There are still rough days. But what was different is that I saw the potential for joy and meaning in my life again. All because of my choice to open myself to the Savior's help. We are not alone.

In many ways, this book is about choices. How we can choose to wake up every morning and feel all of the emotions that we feel because we are human. Just as you can choose to feel your emotions, I believe it's also important to validate them; to accept them. We can choose to deal with the raw and authentic realities of life. This is how we learn to cope.

I've learned to move forward in difficult and trying times, even when I didn't know exactly how it would all work out in the end. If we have a desire to heal and choose to take the necessary steps, we will prevail. If you believe there is a loving God, (and I like to believe that there is), put your trust in the Savior. He is the source of healing. Let His balm in Gilead rinse the sorrow away, and repeat as necessary. We know that pain is unavoidable—essential, even. But even with the presence of pain, love and growth can also exist.

I have come to see the beauty in being open about my struggles, even in the midst of them. It doesn't take away our obstacles, but it takes away the isolation. Any time we bring our struggle out of the darkness and into the light, it sets us up for healing. In our society, perfection seems to be idealized and even obtained—if only on social media—which leaves us all with plenty of room for guilt and shame to creep in. When we open up about our struggles (not necessarily on social media), our vulnerabilities free us from this trap of isolation and shame. That same vulnerability is so critical for our mental and emotional well-being. It allows us to deeply connect with others, validates our feelings, and gives others permission to feel safe in their struggles as well.

Blake made a choice that changed his and many lives forever. But I made choices, too. Choices that changed my life for the better, despite tragedy. I didn't accept the help I needed right at first, but I have found many helpful things since. I started being open with the people around me about what I was struggling with. This began with me journaling my thoughts and feelings. It turned into letting my friends and family into the depths of my heart, and eventually also sharing with strangers who were also struggling. I realized that working with a professional therapist was very beneficial and found that, more than anything, it was a safe space with someone who could help me sort things out for myself.

In the end, I was able to make the choice to forgive Blake, and even more importantly, to forgive myself.

I decided to live every moment.

I decided to heal.

I decided to keep going. And I know you can too.